# JACKIE

The life and times of the most stunning, most talked-about legend living today come alive in this intimate and insightful biography....

- Her socially prominent family and her dashing but troubled father, "Black Jack" Bouvier
- Her first job as inquiring photographer...at $42.50 a week!
- The festive marriage linking her and JFK to such leading social names as Rockefeller, Vanderbilt, Tiffany, DuPont
- Her vastly popular—and ultimately tragic—1,036 days as First Lady
- The incredible strength that got her through the deaths of her infant son Patrick, Robert Kennedy, and Martin Luther King
- Her royal wedding on Ari's private island
- Her frequent battles with—and decisive victories over—the ever-intrusive media
- Her continuing insistence on being her own woman, her own way: beautiful, assertive, dignified.

## A LASTING IMPRESSION

D0921035

# JACKIE
## A LASTING IMPRESSION

Richard Taylor and Sam Rubin

A 2M COMMUNICATIONS LTD.
PRODUCTION

ST. MARTIN'S PRESS/NEW YORK

JACKIE: A LASTING IMPRESSION

Copyright © 1990 by Richard Taylor and Sam Rubin and 2M Communications Ltd.

Photo research by Amanda Rubin.

Cover photograph by Ron Galella.

ISBN: 0-312-91266-8   Can. ISBN: 0-312-91267-6

Printed in the United States of America

First St. Martin's Press mass market edition/January 1990

10  9  8  7  6  5  4  3  2  1

The authors wish to thank the following for their patience and assistance:

Oliver S. Anderson
Debby Doumakes
Vanda Krefft
Stella Jane Mittelbach
Madeleine Morel
Buddy Rubin

For Elizabeth Jean Anderson

If there is a better writer, or a truer friend,
we have yet to meet her.

With love, Sammy and Rick

JACQUELINE BOUVIER ONASSIS HAS HAD THE EXPERIENCE OF MANY LIFETIMES IN HER OWN TIME. HER TWO MARRIAGES, TO A PRESIDENT AND A MULTIMILLIONAIRE, MAKE HER THE world's most intriguing widow. But the true spirit of Jacqueline can only be gleaned by taking her whole life into account. Her childhood and young-adult years before meeting John F. Kennedy, and her exciting and varied life after the death of Aristotle Onassis are also important components in the profile of a truly fascinating woman. Here is the story of a woman of great beauty and courage —a story that makes a lasting impression.

# Chapter One

*A*T THE HEIGHT OF SUMMER IN THE HEIGHT OF AMERICA'S RITZY, GLITZY ROARING TWENTIES, A BABY GIRL WAS born at Long Island's Southampton Hospital. Then as now, Southampton was a favorite summer escape for many of New York City's most wealthy inhabitants. Fresh sea breezes cooled these elite from the humidity and heat of Manhattan. They were people who considered themselves a class apart from most of the world, and they stuck very much together.

The proper entries were made about the baby in the Manhattan society columns: Jacqueline Lee Bouvier joined the world on July 28, 1929. She was an exquisite infant, but that was no surprise. Her mother Janet was beautiful, and her father Jack was drop-dead handsome. The Bouviers were also rich and socially prominent. At their summer home in Southampton, friends and relatives gathered to have a look at their first child, born just a year after their blue-blooded marriage. Gazing at the tiny girl, it would have been easy enough for each of the admiring adults to guess what her future would be: She would grow into a beautiful woman who would marry early into her own social set and settle quietly into a lovely, pampered domestic life where she, in turn, would raise her own children in the same manner.

One of these predictions was quite true. Jacqueline would indeed become a beauty. But not just a Southampton beauty. A world-renowned beauty. The sweet infant who smiled up at them was destined to move far beyond her already enviable beginnings. And those who would know Jacqueline throughout her life might suggest she'd been destined for her future even then.

Not far away, on the summer shores of Massachusetts, a freckled boy of twelve played hard with his brothers and sisters. John was smart, good-looking, and aggressive. He was the kind of kid who could imagine himself running the country one day, except for the fact that his father had already chosen that ambition for his older brother Joe.

But things wouldn't go exactly as planned for these children either. Brother Joe would be killed in World War II, and it would be John Kennedy who would one day make it to the White House, and the baby girl in Southampton who would help him get there.

Much farther from New York, a young man in his early twenties returned to his home in Athens after seven years in Argentina. He had left a poor man and returned rich. But he was not satisfied with what he had. He was determined to be far, far richer still, and with his wealth he would marry whichever woman he most desired. Little did he know, that woman was just now born, and that almost forty years would pass before Aristotle Onassis would see his romantic dream come true.

The first years of Jacqueline's life were spent on Park Avenue in the winters and Southampton in the summers. Certainly this was a child born with a silver spoon in her mouth. On the Bouvier side of the family, Jacqueline was rumored to have been descended from a Frenchman who had fought in the American Revolution. By the early 1800s her relatives were thriving in Philadelphia with a lucrative import business. Later, her grandfather Bouvier became an ambitious and highly successful attorney. The other side of her family—Lee, Jacqueline's middle name, and her mother's maiden name—was newer wealth, but the bank account was impressive just the same.

Even as a little girl Jacqueline had a very strong sense of herself. She was poised and self-possessed beyond her years. Once, when she was four, playing in Central Park while supervised by her nanny, the two accidentally became separated. Jacqueline didn't cry, the way most girls her age would have. While the governess became frantic with worry, she walked calmly around the green until she came upon a policeman. Standing before him, she announced in a clear voice, "My nanny is lost."

Early on, Jacqueline quite clearly saw herself as the center of the world and in full charge whenever she chose to be. This attitude was one that would define her personality for the rest of her life. It would give her strength to survive the tragedies to come, and it would also cause people to call her regal and aloof.

Her father, no doubt, had more to do with his daughter's poise than anyone else. He adored her and showered presents and affection on her without bounds. His marriage was not happy, and for the first three and a half years of his daughter's life, until Lee, a second daughter, was born, Jacqueline was the repository of his love, and she returned hs affection a hundredfold.

Darkly handsome, Jack Bouvier was known as

"Black Jack," and the name was fitting in more than one respect. Although he was dashing and adventurous, he was also an alcoholic and a spendthrift who fought bitterly with his wife and didn't bother to hide his many dalliances with other women.

Black Jack's fond attention to his namesake daughter further distanced him from his wife. As a result, Janet became critical and overbearing with little Jacqueline, who did not accept the bad treatment easily. The problem only became worse when Lee was born. Here was an infant dependent on her mother, someone on whom her mother could dote in return. So Lee became her mother's favorite.

From these early years, Jacqueline and Janet would have an uneasy relationship the rest of their lives. To combat the tension with her mother, Jacqueline kept her focus on her father, to the point where she was years later described by Jack Kennedy as having a "big father crush."

Whatever Black Jack gave her, she cherished, and whatever advice he offered, she took very seriously. Once, he coached her on how to hold other people's attention. Withholding something of yourself, appearing mysterious, was his secret, and he counseled Jacqueline to adopt that stance. Of all the counsel he ever gave her, this certainly was the one that would most affect the way the world later came to see her.

School days began for Jacqueline at the exclusive Chapin School in New York City. It was immediately obvious that she was very bright, and her grades reflected her intelligence. Learning to read was a particularly important event, since books were to become one of her favorite companions throughout the years. Another love—of horses—began early, when, at six, she received her first pony. Other animals also delighted her, and she even persuaded her father to let her keep a pet rabbit for a time in the bathtub of their New York apartment.

In many respects Jacqueline had everything a child could want, but in other ways her life was sorely lacking. It was her misfortune, for instance, that she did not live in a peaceful home. Her father's drinking became worse and his affairs more frequent and more flagrant. With each succeeding year, Janet's anger and bitterness toward her husband increased. Jack had cheated on her during their honeymoon aboard a cruise ship, which devastated her, and though she waited years for him to change, he never did. The couple tried a separation for a time and then were reunited, according to one source, in the interest of the children. But it was no use. In 1940, Janet and Black Jack Bouvier were divorced, and Jacqueline watched her father, the person she loved most in the world, pack up and leave.

For the eleven-year-old, the pain of the broken family was incredible. She felt lonely, frightened, and like many other children who experience divorce, she blamed the parent who remained behind for supposedly driving the absent parent away. Whatever her father might be guilty of, she did not believe it was bad enough to make him leave. This would become an important life lesson for Jacqueline—no matter what the man she married did, she would not drive him away.

If the relationship with her mother had been less than desirable before, it was worse now. And on top of her personal agony, Jacqueline had to face potential embarrassment at school, for in 1940 very few parents in her social circle ever considered divorce. She felt ashamed, withdrew from her group of friends, was no longer interested in the fox-trot dances for children her age held at the Plaza and the St. Regis hotels.

Although they had competed for their father's affection, Jacqueline felt very close to Lee, and she confided her feelings to her sister during that difficult time. Otherwise, Jacqueline chose to be alone. Privacy was the greatest comfort she could give herself. In fact, for the rest of her life, she would turn away from the world at times of tragedy, seeking solitude as a way to regain her strength and to heal.

Two years after the divorce, Janet Bouvier met and married Hugh D. Auchincloss, a Washington broker who had made a sizable fortune. Jacqueline was transferred from the Chapin School to the elite Holton-Arms in Washington, D.C. Gone were the warm, idle days in Southampton. Instead, Jacqueline and Lee would now spend their summers at an estate in Newport, Rhode Island, and the winter months at Merrywood, a château in suburban Virginia. The first thirteen years of life had been elegant for Jacqueline, and life was even more elegant now. Butlers spoke softly as they served elegant meals, and the dinner conversation usually centered on culture and the arts. Jacqueline even had the chance to practice speaking French, which was one of her best subjects in school.

Many looking in from the outside would have believed that Jacqueline had been born a lucky girl and remained one because of all the material possessions surrounding her. However, it was harder to see or measure how much she missed her father, and how strange it seemed to her to have Hugh Auchincloss—kind enough, but so plain, so dull —married to her mother instead. Furthermore, the Auchincloss wealth did not belong to Jacqueline. She was given the necessities, but her stepbrothers and sisters received much, much more.

The writer Gore Vidal, whose mother had been married at an earlier time to Hugh Auchincloss, explained it this way: "Jackie and Lee and I had no money, contrary to what people think. Mr. Auchincloss was very rich...but we were not... That's why I had to work and Jackie and Lee had to marry well." Of course, Jacqueline was too young to marry, but she was old enough and bright enough to understand the financial aspects of her future.

To make matters worse, her maternal grandfather, James Lee, hated his scoundrel son-in-law, Black Jack, so much that he decided to punish Jack for the divorce by denying his own grandchildren his large estate. Jacqueline and Lee were both forced to sign away any and all claims to the Lee estate, effectively disinheriting them.

Jacqueline had just begun adapting to her new life when she was sent off, at age fifteen, to Miss Porter's, a Connecticut boarding school. She was allowed to take her horse, Danseuse, which helped to ease the adjustment. As usual, she was a straight-A student, and soon had the unexpected pleasure of a school-sponsored summer tour of Europe.

It was Jacqueline's first exposure to the world beyond America, and she enjoyed it immensely. She was instantly drawn to art, architecture, and furnishings that dated to times before her nation's existence. Her mind was keen and her memory excellent, and she was henceforth always drawn to things cultural and artistic.

If the people around Jacqueline noticed how intelligent she was, she herself was becoming acutely aware of it, too, and it was making her self-conscious. As a defense, she began to hide behind her soft, girlish voice and a wide-eyed, innocent look. Jonathan Isham, an old friend, recalls taking her to a Yale game when she was still in high school: "She'd say to me, 'Why are they kicking the ball?' ...She felt she ought to play up to the big Yaleman. The truth is, she probably knew more about football than I did."

Like most other high school girls, Jacqueline fretted about getting married while she was still half a child. Once, she confessed to a friend, "I just know no one will marry me, and I'll end up as a house mother at Farmington [Miss Porter's]."

Her worries at sixteen of becoming an old maid were soon dispelled when, at the end of high school, she made her debut. Jacqueline joined the select group of girls whose families had a tradition of formally presenting their daughters when they came of age at eighteen, an introduction to the closed and gilded world of "society." The gala balls at which these young women were put on display were attended by the best-looking, best-dressed, and best-educated men in New York—in other words, men of their own kind. To be a debutante meant that the young woman was deemed ready and eligible for marriage to a young man of the proper standing.

As with her birth, Jacqueline's second, adult arrival into the world was covered by the society columns. And this poised young lady received more attention than any of the other debutantes. She was not only beautiful, but her dark hair, green eyes, and intelligent expression set her beauty apart, as did her reserved manner. So it surprised almost no one when she received the ultimate recognition by being chosen Queen Debutante of the Year. One columnist covering the splendid affair was Igor Cassini, whose brother Oleg would one day become Jacqueline's official White House designer. Igor was duly impressed: "Jacqueline Bouvier [is] a regal debutante who has classic features and the daintiness of a Dresden porcelain."

Jacqueline chose to attend Vassar College, which was not only a socially prominent women's school, but one that had a fine academic standing. As usual, she received straight A's, and never with any toil. Studying history and English literature was a pleasure for her, and learning French, Spanish, and Italian was easy and enjoyable.

Oddly enough, it was the social side of college life that was more difficult for the former Queen Debutante. Boarding at the college meant being separated from her younger sister Lee, her one true confidante. Probably because of her strained relationship with her mother, Jacqueline rarely made close friends with women.

At this time in her life, she was shy with men as well. Young men from Ivy League campuses were immediately attracted to her fabulous looks, but once they had secured a date, they realized they were not in the company of the typical, pretty, marry-me-quick coed. One former date remembers her as "so introverted and shy that it was almost painful to be with her...she was so insecure and complicated." Another, Jonathan Isham, explained, "She had the reputation of being very frigid. She was rather aloof and reserved, but everybody liked her...."

Jacqueline was searching for something beyond what most of those who dated her could offer, and therefore she could not become close to them. In an interview in *Time* magazine shortly after moving into the White House, she explained why she acted differently than her classmates at Vassar: "But Newport—when I was about nineteen, I knew I didn't want the rest of my life to be there. I didn't want to marry any of the young men I grew up with—not because of them, but because of their life. I didn't know what I wanted. I was still floundering."

Very soon, however, she began to find her direction. After two years at Vassar she jumped at the chance to study abroad for a year. She returned to her French roots by choosing the Sorbonne in Paris. In retrospect, it was an experience that would influence her attitudes and taste for years to come. To her stepbrother, Hugh Auchincloss, Jr., she wrote, "It's so different, the feeling you get of the city when you live [here], I thought Paris was all glamour and glitter and rush, but of course it isn't."

Rather, it was a city full of every conceivable art treasure. Much of the world's most exciting art, architecture, literature, and fashion surrounded her every day, and she absorbed it all with the greatest eagerness. Her highly retentive mind took in all the details of fine French furnishings, and her mind's eye recorded the subtle differences between dressed and very, very well dressed. In just a few years she would make this knowledge her own by topping the World's Best Dressed list and by renovating to perfection one of the most famous buildings in the world.

Even in romantic Paris, Jacqueline spent time alone when she could. In the same letter to Hugh, she described her routine: "I really lead two lives —flying to the Sorbonne and Reid Hall—in a lovely, quiet, gray rainy world—or like the maid on her day out—putting on a fur coat and going to the middle of town..."

Jacqueline returned home a changed young woman. Having found in Paris undiscovered trea-

sures, she also made discoveries about herself—
what really interested her in life and what was no
longer important to her. Newspaperman and close
friend Charles Bartlett noticed the difference in
Jacqueline immediately: 'She was no longer the
round little girl who lived next door. She was
more exotic. She had become gayer and livelier."

The first result of this change was her decision
not to return to "being a little girl at Vassar
again." The young ladies at school with her there
were on a very specific course in life, and although
it was a privileged, even pampered course that
many people envied, it was not the one Jacqueline
wanted to follow. So instead, she transferred to
George Washington University in Washington,
D.C. Although she had no particular interest in
politics, George Washington had a less protective
atmosphere. The students were from all back-
grounds in life, and the city itself was a place of
action—the kind of action that affected the entire
world.

Now living in a larger world, Jacqueline was
also more worldly. It was her father, of all people,
who was concerned that she be discreet in whatever she did. In a letter to her addressing the fact
that she had been out all night without good reason, he advised her lovingly that a woman had

nothing if not her reputation. As always, Jacqueline took his words to heart, and remained prudent in her actions thereafter.

She had barely settled into a routine as a student in the nation's capital when fate delivered its next surprise. It came in the form of an invitation to dinner from Charles Bartlett, Washington correspondent for the Chattanooga *Times*. Busy with others things, Jacqueline at first declined, but Bartlett pestered her. There was a very attractive young man he wanted her to meet. He was a Democratic congressman in the House of Representatives, quite an achievement for a man in his early thirties. Bartlett was convinced Jacqueline would like this man named John Kennedy.

From all reports, Jacqueline and Jack got along very well that evening at dinner, although like many married couples, they each remembered the event differently. Later, Jack was to claim that he "leaned across the asparagus and asked for a date." Jacqueline counters this claim by insisting "asparagus was not on the menu."

In any case, the relationship began somewhat slowly at first. Jacqueline was finishing school and had to determine what her career might be. Jack had career concerns too. He was running for the

Senate against a very formidable opponent—Henry Cabot Lodge. If he was to win, he needed to devote almost all of his time to campaigning. Therefore, dates were only occasional, and Jacqueline remembers them with amusement: "He'd call me from some oyster bar up there [in Massachusetts], with a great clinking of coins, to ask me out to the movies the following Wednesday in Washington."

It was the beginning of a casual, all-American courtship, but the destiny that lay ahead for this couple was very far from common.

# Chapter Two

*W*HILE JACK KENNEDY WAS STUMPING TO-
WARD HIS SENATORIAL VICTORY IN
MASSACHUSETTS, JACQUELINE WAS BUSY
forging her own career in Washington, D.C. It was
unusual for a young woman of Jacqueline's social
breeding to go to work after college, but she went
job hunting anyway—not for the money so much
as the excitement and stimulation of being out in
the professional world. As she would be so often
in the future, Jacqueline was ahead of her peers, a
trend setter in accepting the challenge of becoming
a single, working woman.

The position she landed had a unique title if not
a stunning salary. At the Washington *Times-Herald* she was awarded the title of "Inquiring Photographer." For $42.50 a week, she had the job of
photographing people of various walks of life and
asking them questions about themselves. Initially
she had a few technical problems—"I always forgot to pull out the slide"—but they were conquered quickly.

Starting with man-on-the-street and woman-in-
the-supermarket stories, Jacqueline hunted for

people with some kind of spark. "I'd find a bunch of rough, salty characters and ask them about a prizefight just so I could try to capture the way they talked." Years later Jacqueline would use her well-trained ear to poke fun at political opponents and White House sycophants.

After a time, Jacqueline sought more prominent subjects. Working the nation's capital, congressmen and senators were an obvious choice, and she had no trouble at all lining up an interview with the dashing Senator Kennedy, whom she was still dating occasionally, when he had time to leave his home state. Richard Nixon, another President-to-be, also made her list.

Before long Jacqueline was promoted from covering people to covering major news events. Some she even enhanced with her own skilled drawings. Whether she realized it at the time, one of her most significant assignments was President Eisenhower's first inauguration. Could this twenty-two-year-old reporter have guessed that within a few short years she would be standing where Mamie now stood, and the fanfare surrounding her presence as the new First Lady would eclipse completely the excitement of the 1953 event?

Although Jacqueline was gaining valuable experience in a fast-paced, adult world, she wasn't getting rich. Living on her salary plus a fifty dollars a month allowance from her father and occasional extra cash from her mother wasn't easy in a city as expensive as Washington. But she managed by driving a secondhand car and budgeting her funds.

In any case, her lean days were about to end forever. Jacqueline's last professional assignment was to cover the coronation of Queen Elizabeth II. It was a grand extravaganza she was thrilled to behold. And before the year was out, she herself would be the center of a ceremony just as solemn and just as elaborate. A wedding that would captivate the entire world.

During her brief, successful career, Jacqueline enjoyed another honor which was well-earned. She entered *Vogue* magazine's Prix de Paris fashion/writing contest and won. Outdoing 1280 other women, she received a wonderful prize indeed—a return trip to her beloved Paris.

One question each competitor had to answer was which three famous men they would most like to meet. Jacqueline's answer gave an insight into her mature personality and extremely refined tastes. She chose: 1) Oscar Wilde, the sharp-witted British playwright and socialite; 2) Diaghilev, the world-renowned Russian ballet choreographer; and 3) Baudelaire, France's greatest poet. She was a young woman whose knowledge and appreciation of a wide range of the arts and cultures far exceeded that of her peers.

Thrilled as she was to win the prize, Jacqueline declined the wonderful trip due to pressure from her mother. For years now, it seemed, Janet found one way or another to disapprove of many of Jacqueline's actions or plans. So Jacqueline remained in the States and kept busy with a new man in her life—another John—John Husted, Jr. In fact, within a short time Husted and Jacqueline were engaged.

A nice-looking Yale man with good social standing, John was the kind of fellow that the young women of Jacqueline's background almost always married. Janet approved of these qualities in John, but frowned upon his income. As a broker beginning his career in New York, he made a mere $17,000 a year, and his prospects for future income were not guaranteed. As a result, Jacqueline's mother formally objected to the match.

For a time Jacqueline held her ground about the engagement. She even took Husted to meet Black Jack, since his approval was of utmost importance to her. Husted recalls the meeting and asking for Jacqueline's hand. Black Jack was charming, but also disarmingly honest: "Sure—but it will never work." That was the only conversation Husted ever had with Mr. Bouvier.

The engagement to Husted was announced officially with a socially correct party at the Auchincloss estate. Jacqueline's ring was sapphire and diamonds, and the couple appeared very happy, particularly Husted, who was crazy about his bride-to-be. Years later he still remembered her with great fondness: "I loved Jackie and wanted very much to marry her ... She was a delight; very free-minded, quite smart, and had a very good sense of humor."

After the party, Husted returned to this job in Manhattan and he and his fiancée began corresponding and arranging ways that they could have time together. But according to Husted, the tone of Jacqueline's letters grew cooler and cooler with time. Even as she planned the wedding and visited the priest, she also was seeing Jack Kennedy, and finally mentioned it to Husted.

The final break came quite undramatically, at the Washington airport. Jacqueline met Husted's plane one weekend and returned the ring. There were no tears and no recriminations. Inwardly, Husted was heartbroken, but for Jacqueline the dissolution was easier. She was deeply in love with John Kennedy, and by now she knew he was the one she wanted to spend her life with.

While Jacqueline was ending her relationship with Husted, John Kennedy was also reassessing his life. Having triumphed over Henry Cabot Lodge for the Massachusetts Senate seat, Kennedy now believed more than ever that he had a very good chance of soon becoming President. He was personally very popular with voters, and so were most of his policies. Kennedy's father, Joseph Sr., was an impressively wealthy man who could contribute enormous amounts of money to his son's campaigns and who understood the machinations of American politics at their most effective, if not always their most scrupulous.

Joe Kennedy, Sr. had an overriding ambition—even larger than his desire to make money—of putting one of his sons in the White House. Upon the death of his first born, Joe Jr., this powerful patriarch transferred his dream to John and placed it squarely on his shoulders. John Kennedy turned out to be the perfect heir to his father's aspirations. He was every bit a match for his father in energy and determination. Together they were an unbeatable team. In 1953 the question was: What else did John need to do to groom himself for a presidential candidacy?

An answer came quickly to them—John needed a wife. The American public would accept a dashing bachelor for a senator, but it would not entrust the most important job in the nation to someone who appeared so boyish.

The next question was: Who should he marry?

John had always liked women, so much so that no one could keep up with his various affairs. But one thing people who knew Jack could all attest to was that he loved voluptuous women, particularly pretty ones who had a public image—models and actresses. The one woman, they noticed, who seemed to be the exception to Jack's pattern was Jacqueline Bouvier, whom he dated intermittently. With her, Jack learned to tolerate fox hunting and Ingmar Bergman movies. Another difference was that Jacqueline had blue-blooded breeding and the other women didn't.

Thus it was no surprise that Joe Sr. actively encouraged John's relationship with Jacqueline. Coming from an Irish-immigrant background that was never socially accepted in Boston, Joe taught his sons that it was imperative to "marry up" the social ladder. The lesson was simple—the women you date are not always the right kind of woman to marry. Jacqueline was definitely the marrying kind.

Having lived the freewheeling single life for so long, Jack needed a little time to make his decision about Jacqueline. In fact, he talked it over so often with his friends that they began to kid him that he should have Congress vote on it. Father Joe pointed out that with her Auchincloss name, she would bring to the Kennedys a connection through marriage to some of America's social leaders, including the Rockefellers, Vanderbilts, Tiffanys, and Du Ponts.

For her part, Jacqueline had no hesitation about marrying Jack. She was clearly in love with him, and it was easy to understand why. Jack Kennedy was in so many ways a replica of the father she worshiped. Both Jack and Black Jack were charming womanizers, handsome and fun. They made Jacqueline feel happy and special when she was with them, and in addition, John Kennedy had an air of tremendous confidence that balanced Jacqueline's natural shyness. When Kennedy finally proposed in June 1953, Jacqueline couldn't have felt happier. At just this time the *Saturday Evening Post* was doing a story on John called "the Senate's Gay Young Bachelor," and news of the engagement was not released until after the article appeared. She might have thought she was walking through a fairy tale as she accepted a ring from America's most eligible man.

Jacqueline's mother wasn't pleased with the Kennedy social standing, but she looked very favorably upon their huge fortune. As for Black Jack, he liked the young senator very much and was all for the union. Jacqueline always liked to remember their first meeting: "They were very much alike. We three had dinner and they talked about politics, sports, and girls—what all red-blooded men talk about." So it was a happy family all around on June 25, when Janet Auchincloss announced the engagement.

Immediately the nation took notice. The press appeared, and for the next ten years their collective interest in this handsome couple would remain unquenchable. *Life* magazine followed Jack and Jacqueline to the Kennedy home in Hyannis Port and supplied the country with pictures of the new celebrities playing softball and lounging on the veranda. The article was entitled, "Life Goes Courting with a U.S. Senator."

This was Jacqueline's first exposure to the press and the public at large, so her husband-to-be, already a public figure, was more squarely the center of attention. But not for long. With each passing year, Jacqueline would garner more and more fanfare without even trying, until finally she would surpass her husband in fame and celebrity. During the *Life* interview, Jacqueline admitted lightly that "we hardly ever talk politics." It was true, and as time passed, this would become a source of conflict between them. But for now, life was very rosy, or at least mostly rosy.

If Jacqueline had one complaint about her fiancé, it was his family—and how much time he liked to spend with them. She had come from a small, broken home and now found herself in a large, cohesive one. Having had a lot of individual attention from both of her parents, Jacqueline didn't like the way the individuals in the Kennedy family were subsumed by the group.

For a soft-spoken woman from a family of two children, the Kennedy clan was overwhelming both in numbers and volume. It was a family of boisterous overachievers who liked to play rough sports and talk tough politics. This went for the women as much as the men. Joe Kennedy had raised his children this way and was proud of them: "Competition—that's what makes them go ...They're all competitive, including the girls."

Jacqueline had never liked team sports, but she

made an attempt to join in the summer games at Cape Cod, until John's younger brother Teddy accidentally broke her ankle during touch football. To an interviewer she explained, "Just watching them tires me out." But privately she was more extreme in her comments to her sister Lee and to friends: "They'll kill me before I ever get to marry him. I swear they will."

The Kennedy women were particularly difficult for Jacqueline to adjust to. They spoke loudly and were quick to poke fun. Ethel, Bobby's wife, laughed at Jacqueline's size-ten feet and called them clodhoppers. Behind Jacqueline's back the women called her "the Debutante" and had a good time imitating her soft, childlike voice.

In return, Jacqueline called Eunice, Ethel, and Jean "the rah-rah girls" and described Ethel as "the type who would put a slipcover on a Louis Quinze sofa and then spell it Luie Cans."

As the summer progressed, Jacqueline put her foot down about how often she would have dinner at the raucous table in Hyannis Port. Not every night, she told Jack. Once or twice a week would be plenty. Oddly enough, it was the overbearing patriarch, Joe, who quickly became Jacqueline's favorite. And Joe liked her just as much in return. He admired her strength of character and sharp wit. She could hold her own with little more than a whisper. Once, at the family table when Jack asked her for a penny for her thoughts, she replied: "But they're my thoughts, Jack, and they would not be my thoughts anymore if I told you, now would they?"

Jack was rendered speechless, but Joe was delighted, saying, "By God, Jack, she's got zipperoo. Jackie's a girl with a mind of her own...."

Joe's comment was not lost on his clan. The more approval he showed of Jacqueline, the more the others came to accept her as she was rather than expecting her to become like them. Over time they would all become quite attached to her, but no one more than Joe. Until the day of his death, Joe remained one of Jacqueline's most beloved.

The wedding to end all weddings was set for September, and that meant a lot of feverish planning through the short summer months. Jacqueline found it necessary to give up her job in order to plan her trousseau and help her mother with the details of the ceremony. Janet Auchincloss wanted an elegant but quiet affair. After the publicity over the engagement, she told her future son-in-law that she preferred something far more private for the wedding ceremony: "No press, no pictures, just a discreet notice in the Newport papers." Kennedy laughed and reminded her that he was a U.S. senator, and as such, a news item. One of the many things that Jacqueline liked about John was the offhand way in which he stood up to her mother. Jack, it seemed, would win every time.

And so did his father, Joe. Although traditionally the wedding plans are left to the bride's family, Joe saw this as a political occasion as much as a social one, and he was determined to have it play to his son's best advantage. He stepped in and took control of the guest lists, the logistics, and the nuptial mass.

Jacqueline had been baptized a Catholic, her father's religion, but she received very little religious training growing up. In addition, both her mother and Hugh Auchincloss were Protestant. So it was no surprise that Janet protested when Joe wanted to turn the wedding ceremony into a highly Catholic affair. She didn't mind having a priest say the mass, but Joe had bigger ideas. Archbishop Cushing, an old Kennedy ally, agreed to be the main celebrant. Attending with him would be a monsignor and four priests. Several other distinguished clergy were to be present on the altar as cocelebrants. As one family member recalls, "Janet was fit to be tied." But there was very little she could do about it except give Joe Kennedy the leeway he wanted.

The Auchincloss guest list comprised a moderate number of socially important people. The Kennedy list, on the other hand, was unbelievable. Movie stars and politicians were favorites. As Janet selected the menu for the luncheon reception and ordered the best champagne, the list of invitees grew and grew, until it reached a whopping nine hundred! Knowing there would be a mob of press and spectators, Joe even arranged for a police cordon. And, last but not least, he commissioned the cake, a four-foot-high confectioner's delight.

Leaving the wedding particulars to the others, JFK kept his attention on his Senate obligations and also arranged for a brief trip to Europe—a last bachelor fling. From all accounts, Jack was not faithful to his fiancée during their engagement, nor after their marriage either. He didn't make much effort to cover his tracks, nor was he serious about the women with whom he spent time. If Jacqueline knew of his last-minute bachelor flings, she didn't let on. No doubt her father's Casanova habits had her well prepared for such behavior.

September 12, 1953, was a lovely, early fall day, and the six hundred people who crowded into St.

Mary's Church looked very happy to be there. Jacqueline carried a bouquet of pink orchids to match the pink taffeta gowns of her twelve bridesmaids. John was a Gaelic prince in his formal attire and deep tan. When Mr. and Mrs. John F. Kennedy emerged from the church over an hour later, nearly two thousand spectators were on hand simply to look at the blessed couple. One guest would later describe the scene as "just like the coronation."

In fact, that was a very apt description. These two stunning young people were as close to royalty as America would ever come. The White House was a few difficult years ahead, but already the nation was bequeathing Jack and Jacqueline its very special attention. Everyone agreed, this spectacle was outdoing even the Astor wedding some twenty years before.

The reception at Auchincloss's Hammersmith Farm followed. *Life* magazine led the press coverage, and several hundred additional guests joined those who had witnessed the taking of vows. The receiving line was so long that it took over two hours for the guests to give their best wishes to the bride and groom. Never had Jacqueline been more ravishing than on this day, in her off-the-shoulder bridal gown, a single strand of choker pearls at her neck. As would become her fashion mark, she managed to combine simplicity and elegance for a breathtaking effect. To see the mob of onlookers that police held back at the edge of the estate's long driveway, she might have been a famous movie star.

During the reception toasts, Jacqueline had the wittiest moment of the day. Explaining that her mother had taught her that one could understand a lot about a man through his correspondence, she held up a postcard for all to see. The picture was of a passion flower, and Jack had sent it to her from an island resort. The message was brief: "Wish you were here. Cheers. Jack." Jacqueline understood her husband well: "This is my entire correspondence from Jack." The guests roared and Jack gave Jacqueline a big smile. Here was the wit he so much appreciated.

But amidst all the festivities, there was one piece out of place, although almost no one seemed to notice. Dear Black Jack was not present. It had been Hugh Auchincloss who had walked his step-daughter down the aisle, because her own father was in a nearby hotel room, too drunk to walk. Accounts vary as to what happened. At this time in his life Black Jack had become an alcoholic, so the reason for his failure could have been that simple. However, Janet had been at war with her former husband over his attendance—she had first begged and then ordered him to stay away. When he insisted on his right to give his own daughter away, some insiders believe that she took matters into her own hands by arranging with the hotel staff to supply him with booze until he was too drunk to function. Whatever the truth of that day, it was a deep and sharp pain for Jacqueline.

While she had changed into her gray traveling suit, and she and Jack were showered with rose petals as they descended the sweeping staircase of Hammersmith Farm, her father was taken to a hospital to treat his severe drunkenness. Jacqueline's consolation was the man whose arm she held. He was the closest she would ever come to replicating her beloved father, and no matter what troubles came between them in the future, she would never stop loving him. If life is never perfect, she had found something that was very close.

# Chapter Three

HE HONEYMOON WAS SPLENDID—A YOUNG BRIDE'S DREAM. JACQUELINE WAS GLAD THAT THEY HAD CHOSEN ACApulco, far from the many distractions of their busy routines. The sun-drenched Mexican resort was the perfect place for them to relax and truly enjoy one another. For the first time since she had met John Kennedy, she had his undivided attention.

If Jacqueline had been happy as a fiancée, she was probably even happier as a new bride. John was everything he appeared to be: handsome, sexy, intelligent, and fun. In all the years to come, Jacqueline's only public complaint about her husband would be that she never had enough time with him.

Returning to the States, Mr. and Mrs. Kennedy settled into their new life as a married couple. Jack suggested they live at Hyannis Port for the time being. He was terribly busy with his Senate duties and didn't want the extra pressure of setting up a new household right away.

But there were pressures for Jacqueline nonetheless. Not only was she surrounded with the overwhelming Kennedy clan, but she was now a national politician's wife, and there was nothing in her past to prepare her for this. As she explained herself, "Being married to a senator, you have to adjust to the fact that the only routine is no routine. He is never at home before seven forty-five or eight, often later. He's away almost every weekend, making a speech somewhere. No, I don't go along. I stay home. And he's usually so tired that only about once a week are we able to go out—or have someone in."

To have someone in wasn't always easy either. In fact, there were times when Jacqueline was the last to know that she was giving a party. "One morning the first year we were married, Jack said to me, 'What food are you planning for the forty guests we are having for luncheon?' No one had told me anything about it. It was eleven A.M. and the guests were expected at one. I was in a panic."

When they did entertain in their home, it was difficult for the couple to settle on a menu, the kind of guests, or the subjects of conversation. Jack loved to talk back-room politics with other politicos over simple all-American food. Jacqueline liked intimate gatherings with fine French cuisine served to friends who enjoyed discussing art and literature. The couple couldn't even share the books they read. While Jack loved to delve into history books, Jacqueline preferred good fiction, like the French novelist Colette.

Unfortunately, the newlyweds' problems were not limited to the dining room. Not only did they lack common interests and time alone together, they had a difficult time relating to one another's feelings. Jack had never been an overtly emotional or affectionate person, and he admitted as much. "I just can't do it," he once explained. For Jacqueline, who had always been such a private person, it was not much easier. Therefore, when the inevitable problems of marriage arose, they had a tough time working them out.

To add to their other troubles, Jacqueline became pregnant soon after the wedding but miscarried the child. To lose a baby is a great disappointment to any woman, but as a Kennedy, there was an even greater pressure for Jacqueline to have children. As Catholics in the 1950s, the Kennedys believed strongly in large families, and it was the woman's main duty as a wife to bear and raise as many children as possible. John's young brother Bobby and his wife Ethel already had half a dozen offspring, and there were more to come.

However, if the clan believed that Jacqueline wasn't quite a Kennedy in her interests and actions, they soon reconsidered. All her life, Jacqueline's reserve would confuse people—they couldn't be sure what she was thinking. During the first months of her marriage, she set the record straight for them all. She wrote a poem to Jack fashioned after Stephen Vincent Benet's "The Midnight Ride of Paul Revere." Each line, each stanza, proved how much she really understood and respected her husband, his heritage, and his ambitions.

Nothing could have delighted Jack more than this ode to him, so much so, that he wanted to publish it. But Jacqueline insisted that it be kept privately between them. Jack complied, but he couldn't resist showing it off to his parents and brothers and sisters. They, too, were very impressed. Even Rose, Jacqueline's mother-in-law, was taken in. She had always been quite cool toward Jacqueline, but now her feelings changed. It would be she who would years later publish the poem as part of her memoirs, admitting that while the Kennedys had had some negative views of Jacqueline, "among one or another of Jack's brothers and sisters or cousins at first, they were immediately resolved when they read that marvelous poem."

In other, more surface ways, JFK and his wife gradually came to understand and accommodate one another. Because her husband liked history, Jacqueline enrolled in a refresher class in American History at Georgetown University. She also took up golf and waterskiing, two sports Jack enjoyed. And at his request, she cut down her cigarette smoking. In return, Jack learned to appreciate continental cuisine and to take direction from his wife in dressing. Because they were each iron-willed individuals with proud self-images, the adjustments took time, but they were achieved.

As they worked on truly becoming a couple, Jack and Jacqueline soon found themselves confronted with challenges beyond the ordinary. Despite Jack's vigorous, athletic appearance, he had serious health problems. For years he had suffered from back problems which had recently become worse. Additionally, he endured Addison's disease, a failure of the adrenal glands, which causes a general weakness and low blood pressure as well as a brownish discoloration of the skin.

By 1955, JFK's condition was so bad that he was using crutches to walk and trying to bear up under constant pain. The only solution his New York doctors could offer was an operation to fuse his spine. The procedure was not guaranteed to work, and in Jack's case there was a considerable risk that he might die on the operating table because of his adrenal problem. Jack thought the operation was worth the chance, saying, "I'd rather be dead than spend the rest of my life on these goddamn crutches."

Jacqueline bravely supported her husband's decision, but she couldn't help being apprehensive. In this case her fears were well founded. The operation did not succeed, and even worse, a life-threatening infection set in and John became delirious and then comatose. A priest was called to the hospital to give him the last rites, and his family gathered around him. Jacqueline had never before been particularly religious, but she prayed now with all her heart.

Amazingly, JFK did regain consciousness. But beyond that, he was still a very sick man. Jacqueline was at his side constantly as his consolation and his entertainment. Speaking of that time, she said quite simply, "It was horrible." Jack was no longer in critical condition, but his back pain was excruciating, and so in early 1956 he chose to undergo a second operation. This time the procedure was a success. His recovery, however, would be months in coming.

Jack was restless and worried about his Senate responsibilities, so he and Jacqueline decided to wait out his convalescence at the Kennedy home in Florida as a way to take his mind off his worries. He had a room overlooking the pool, but it made little difference to a man who had to remain flat on his back and could not even enjoy the comfort of a pillow. Of course, Jacqueline wanted to help, but there was little she could do. Later she explained, "I think convalescence is harder to bear than great pain." At least that seemed to be true for her husband, who was growing increasingly despondent.

What saw them through this trying time was Jack's idea for writing a book and Jacqueline's indispensable help in assisting with the project. It would be called *Profiles in Courage* and would contain a number of short histories on the courageous acts of famous men. The project required plenty of research and reading, and Jacqueline did plenty of both for her husband, including reading aloud to him when he was too fatigued to hold a book. Not only did the project take Jack's mind off his pain, but it brought new life to the house. Aides arrived from Washington to give extra support, and there was a constant stream of letters and phone calls as Jack gathered the information he needed.

Now that he was active mentally again, Jack felt back in touch with the world and his spirits rose. His ambitions returned, stronger than ever. The 1956 presidential race loomed not far ahead, and Jack knew he wanted to be on the Democratic ticket. His real desire was the presidency, but he agreed with his advisers that he would probably be viewed as too young and inexperienced. So instead he would go after the number-two position.

After many months of writing, the book was complete, and during that time, Jack solidified his new political plans. With each passing week he gained strength until finally he was walking without crutches, ready and eager to return to Washington. Jacqueline realized how their time together would be affected by a national campaign, but she had also learned during her months in Florida that her husband could never be a happy man unless he was striving toward greatness. If she truly loved him, she had to allow him to follow his life's course, and she determined that she was woman enough to do that.

Back in Washington, Senator Kennedy was met with warm fanfare from constituents and the press. Jacqueline laughed with him about the attention: "God. It was like recording the Crown Prince taking his first baby steps."

Feeling renewed and optimistic, the couple decided it was time to buy their own home. Jacqueline found the house she wanted—a white-brick Georgian called Hickory Hill. She was drawn to this place for several reasons. First of all, it was very close to Merrywood, where she had spent part of her childhood. It also was a building of historical significance, which she valued. During the Civil War it had served as a general's headquarters. Most importantly, however, it had a lovely room that was perfect for a nursery. Mr. and Mrs. Kennedy were expecting a child again.

By now Jacqueline had been fully accepted by the Kennedy clan, and accepted on her own terms. Ironically, they came to respect her for holding her own rather than changing her personality to become like them, displaying a strength of character they all admired.

Among the qualities the family appreciated in Jacqueline was her gift-giving habits. They had learned to look forward to her presents at special occasions. All of her life, Jacqueline would be a generous and original present buyer, putting much more time and thought into her selection than most people ever do. She liked to choose beautifully bound, precious books, for instance—something that had not been unwrapped much before in the Kennedy household.

Also, she was painting again—happy, primitive pictures which were very good—and the family came to appreciate her talent.

Jacqueline was not planning to be much involved in Jack's campaign, though no one could have supported him more in spirit. The reason she gave was, "Jack wouldn't—couldn't—have a wife who shared the spotlight with him." Nor was she consulted about issues, nor did she wish to be. Nonetheless, with each passing year she would be more and more in the spotlight, whether she chose to or not.

The 1956 Democratic convention was held in Chicago. As could have been expected, the city was hot and muggy when the Kennedy clan arrived for last-minute, intense campaigning. A very pregnant Jacqueline spent most of the time behind the scenes, giving her husband confident moral support. Kennedy was in competition was Estes Kefauver for the position as Adlai Stevenson's running mate. The Kennedy team was large, well-financed, and thorough. The groundwork had all been laid, and hopes were high for his nomination to the ticket.

Thus were they all stunned and unprepared for the third-ballot defeat that gave the honor to Kefauver instead. After the shattering decision, Kennedy left the convention hall and met Jacqueline and his good friend Senator George Smathers, who likened the group's mood to a wake. Jack telephoned his father, who was in the French Riviera. Nothing could have been harder than telling Joe, his biggest supporter, about the outcome. "We did our best, Dad," is about all he could say. Jacqueline did her best to console him, but he could not be comforted.

The following day, Jack was still so upset that he decided to leave for the Riviera immediately to join his father and get a break from the American political scene. Because Jacqueline was nearly due, and because she disliked flying at any time, she did not want to accompany him and begged him not to go. So absorbed was he in his own disappointment, that he disregarded her request and set off immediately for France, leaving her behind.

Jacqueline had been abandoned once before by the man she loved—when her father left home in her childhood—and perhaps she felt the panic of abandonment again. In any case, those close to her at the time realized that she was extremely upset when she left Chicago and went to stay with the Auchinclosses at Hammersmith Farm. One friend who was with her at the time remembers it well: "...she was so upset by him taking off like that, she turned herself inside out, letting it eat away at her..." The result was that within a week Jacqueline was hospitalized for an emergency cesarean. The baby was a girl—stillborn.

It was Bobby Kennedy who joined Jacqueline at the hospital to support her in her grief, just as it would be Bobby who would be her strength through so many harrowing times in the future. In the meantime, word spread quickly to the newspapers, which proclaimed: SENATOR KENNEDY ON MEDITERRANEAN TRIP UNAWARE HIS WIFE HAS LOST BABY. Other Kennedys were busy trying to track down Jack. It was three days before they found him and he returned to Washington. But soon after the baby was buried, Jack left again, this time hitting the campaign trail for his party—the

Stevenson/Kefauver ticket. Once again, Jacqueline was left alone.

Happiness lay ahead, for she would be a mother sooner than she thought. First, however, there was another loss for Jacqueline to bear, although this time she had some warning. In 1957, Black Jack Bouvier's drinking caught up with him and his liver began to fail. He was dying, and both he and his daughter knew it. But he also knew that she was pregnant again, and this pleased him tremendously. What Jacqueline wanted in the summer of '57 was for her father to live long enough to see his first grandchild, who was due in December. But Black Jack had less time than either of them realized, and just after Jacqueline's twenty-eighth birthday, he died.

The funeral was held at St. Patrick's Cathedral in New York, and Jacqueline made all the arrangements herself. She chose meadow flowers to decorate the altar rather than more formal and therefore more somber floral arrangements. Unfortunately, very few people showed up for Black Jack's service. He had been a friend and lover to so many, but somehow he had lost track of them or they of him. About all that Black Jack left behind in the world was an estate of less than $200,000, which his daughters divided.

Jacqueline found therapy for her sadness in the new house she was planning to move into. After the death of her last child, she did not want to put her new baby in the nursery at Hickory Hill. So she and Jack bought a place in Georgetown on a tree-lined street with a lovely enclosed garden at the rear. She decided to redecorate in the eighteenth-century French tradition that was by now her favorite. The high walls were painted pink, and inlaid tables displayed delicate French clocks. Visitors were offered a seat on Louis Quinze chairs.

Caroline Bouvier Kennedy was born on schedule, a healthy, perfect baby. Jacqueline finally had so much of what she wanted. She told a magazine interviewer, "I love to read, love to paint, love my house and my baby. I like gardening, but I'm not very good at it. I'm better at arranging flowers."

The other thing Jacqueline was good at arranging was her busy household. An organized person by nature, she was even more so now. She not only supervised her child and her hired help, but looked after her husband as well. "I brought a certain amount of order to his life," she admitted. "We had good food in our house —not merely the bare staples that he used to have...he got to the airport without a mad rush because I packed for him...It's those little things that make you tired." Her own wardrobe was also meticulously arranged, and she never lost sight of her overall schedule.

There were certain things, however, that Jacqueline couldn't arrange, and one was her husband's ferocious energy and ambition. He had recovered from the defeat at the '56 convention and was ready to try again, this time for the presidency. Always Jack had pushed himself hard toward his goals, but now he was relentless. Jacqueline had never spent as much time with him as she had wanted, but from 1958 to 1960 their time together was even more abbreviated. She couldn't help but feel lonely, and later described that period as "wrong, all wrong."

Luckily, she had little Caroline for company. Although the child had a full-time nanny named Maud Shaw, Jacqueline spent hours and hours with Caroline herself, reading to her and taking her for walks in the park.

As for women friends, Jacqueline didn't have many, and that seemed to be the way she liked it. She didn't feel much interested in groups of ladies or the activities they engaged in. She once said sarcastically, "Mummy thinks the trouble with me is that I don't play bridge with my bridesmaids."

Jacqueline may have been understanding about her time apart from her husband, but Washington social circles and the press were not. Rumors ignited that the Kennedys were in trouble, that divorce loomed. *Time* magazine went so far as to publish a story claiming that Joe Kennedy was paying Jacqueline one million dollars not to leave John. There was not much proof to the claim, but when the subject was JFK or his wife, people were willing to talk whether they had the facts or not. John was said to have dozens of affairs while he was away on political business. Left behind, Jacqueline also was seen with other men, who were serving as her escorts in place of her absent husband. In the face of all the gossip, Jacqueline felt helpless. "What can I do? I have dinner with someone...get photographed with someone without Jack—and then everyone automatically says, 'Oh, he must be her new lover.' How can you beat that?"

Those who knew Jacqueline well no doubt realized that the divorce rumors were not true. Even if Jack were unfaithful to her, it was unlikely that she would leave him, since her own adored father had been the same way. She had grown up with such behavior and probably accepted it as a normal, if sometimes hurtful, part of marriage.

And almost certainly it did hurt. Jacqueline had always been given to moodiness, and during this period in her life her emotions were heavily taxed. Jack, on the other hand, was quite even-tempered, and didn't quite understand her more mercurial nature. For her part, she greatly admired his steadiness. "He is a rock, and I lean on him in everything. He is so kind. Ask anyone who works for him. And he's never irritable or sulky."

Whatever rift there may have been between them began to close at the start of the 1960 presidential primaries. JFK was in the national spotlight as never before, and if he were to win the election, he needed the presence and cooperation of his wife. As luck would have it, Jacqueline was pregnant again. Everyone on the Kennedy campaign realized that this would limit her ability to follow him on the trail, but she was willing to do whatever her strength and health would allow. She recognized the alternative: "If Jack didn't run for President, he'd be like a tiger in a cage."

One of her biggest jobs at the time was simply

staying abreast of her husband's impossibly demanding schedule. Early on, she explained what she knew lay ahead: "He'll be going, going, going constantly, and I'll be absolutely worn out just trying to keep track of him." She accompanied him to the first, key primaries, and even took over his speaking duties in Wisconsin when he was called back to Washington briefly. Whether she liked the duties or not, she proved herself quite capable.

Because Jack was only forty-two at the time, there was still much talk about his being too young to hold the highest office in the land. Reporters and fellow Democrats often asked him if he would accept the vice-presidential nomination instead, if it came to that. Jack had tried for second place last time and lost it all. This time he was determined to seek only his heart's true desire—to be President of the United States. Jacqueline understood his sentiments and felt the same way herself. Although she rarely spoke up on political matters, she voiced her opinion quite clearly on this issue: "If you don't believe Jack, I'll cut my wrists and write an oath in blood that he'll refuse to run with Stevenson."

The Democratic convention was held in Los Angeles in 1960. Jacqueline chose to remain at home in Washington, perhaps in part due to the bad memories she associated with the previous convention. But the outcome this time couldn't have been better. Jack won over 760 delegates. With Lyndon Johnson as his running mate, he stood before his party and received their tumultuous cheers.

That night there was a wild victory party hosted by Jack's sister Pat and her husband, actor Peter Lawford, at their home nearby. There was skinny-dipping and drinking and plenty of noise, and finally the police arrived to check on the disturbance. It wasn't until the boisterous guests were taken to the station that the police realized that they had a presidential nominee on their hands. If the police were worried, they didn't need to be. Accounts have it that Jack laughed uproariously at the whole affair.

Jacqueline, on the other hand, took a more sober approach to the victory. At her first press meeting, she made it clear that her support for her husband was a hundred percent: "I suppose I won't be able to play much part in the campaign, but I'll do what I can. I feel I should be with Jack when he's engaged in such a struggle, and if it weren't for the baby, I'd campaign even more vigorously than Mrs. Nixon."

Behind the scenes, Jack didn't expect much campaign work from his wife. He knew she looked terrific, and that in itself was a major contribution. As usual, he urged her to keep her smoking to a minimum. Beyond that, he recommended, "Just smile a lot and talk about Caroline."

Even so, Jack underestimated his wife's appeal. From the day he was nominated, the press began to speculate about a White House with a First Lady who was just past thirty. If she thought she was going to be in the background of this campaign, it didn't turn out that way. The public loved any detail they could learn about her, and the more pictures, the better. She was young, strikingly beautiful, elegantly dressed, and highly intelligent. What more could a country ask of a woman who would represent them?

Her wardrobe was particularly interesting to the media. She was one of the first to wear a "sack" dress and to streak her hair and have it done in a bouffant style. If she was seen in bright, colored slacks, or without socks and shoes while strolling the neighborhood, it was covered like a news item. She was photographed sailing, painting, and playing with Caroline. How would she decorate the White House? people wanted to know. Who would she entertain there? The historic house, she assured the press, would not be turned into a modern building. "The White House is an eighteenth- and nineteenth-century house, and should be kept as a period house." As for entertaining, she had always been inclined toward intimate gatherings, a style that would most likely continue if she were First Lady.

Not all of the attention was so pleasant. Gossip columnists started rumors that Jacqueline was not actually pregnant and only pretended to be to avoid the rigors of campaigning. *Women's Wear Daily* claimed she spent $30,000 a year on French clothing. Jacqueline shot down this statement with her characteristic wit, saying she couldn't spend that much, "even if I wore sable underwear." But her remark was quoted so often that it only enhanced the controversy.

What this all had to do with politics might not have been immediately obvious, but it was nonetheless important to the outcome of the election. Because Jack was running against Richard Nixon, Jacqueline was in essence running against Pat Nixon. Mrs. Nixon had come from a modest background, and so had her husband. They attended ordinary schools and worked extremely hard to get as far as they had come. In fact, Pat's wages as a schoolteacher had helped finance her husband's first campaign. Now, Mrs. Nixon left her two daughters at home and stumped the nation with her husband. Also, Pat was a number of years older than Jacqueline, conservative in her dress, and although attractive enough, not the beauty Jacqueline was.

When America went to the polls in November 1960, it decided between two men and their differing domestic and foreign policies. But it also was selecting an image for itself as a nation, deciding how it wanted to see itself for the next four years. If America wanted a new accent on youth, with beauty and elegance and refinement thrown in, Kennedy was the ticket and Jacqueline was the symbol.

On Election Day, Jacqueline Kennedy voted for the first time in her life. She voted only for the office of President, because, she jokingly said, "I didn't want to dilute it by voting for anyone else." Not surprisingly, she voted for John Kennedy, and so did a majority across the country. At three A.M. Richard Nixon appeared on television to concede. The senator from Massachusetts would be America's next leader.

In characteristic Kennedy fashion, John greeted the next day, the day of his official victory, by playing touch football with the rest of his family at Hyannis Port. Already Secret Service men were on detail and the press thronged around the yard. For a time they almost didn't notice the solitary figure in a raincoat walking off alone down the beach. It was Jacqueline. She had been an integral part of the victory, but now she chose to remove herself from the celebration. She needed time to think, to adjust. Was she ready to be First Lady? Was she ready to stand beside the most powerful man in the world? She knew one thing: She had never aspired to this—destiny had put her here.

# Chapter Four

*J*ACQUELINE'S WALK ON THE SAND WAS ONE OF THE LAST PRIVATE-CITIZEN MOMENTS SHE WOULD ENJOY FOR YEARS TO COME. LITERALLY OVERNIGHT, THE ROUTINE OF HER home life changed utterly. Her stately, quiet Georgetown home turned before her eyes into the temporary headquarters of the next American administration—the world's most powerful government. The once spacious house was suddenly bursting at the seams with people, some of them strangers. Jacqueline couldn't go from one room to the next without encountering Secret Service agents and political aides. Trying to joke about the situation, she explained, "I could be in the bathroom, in the tub, and then find that Pierre Salinger was holding a press conference in my bedroom!" She couldn't step outside away from the rush of activity for even a moment without being confronted by reporters and assaulted by bright TV lights. As delighted as she was at her husband's achievement, Jacqueline found the adjustment difficult, particularly at eight months pregnant: "I feel as though I have just turned into a piece of public property. It's really frightening to lose your anonymity at thirty-one."

Whether Jacqueline realized it or not, a good deal of the commotion was due to her. She had become a unique kind of celebrity the day she got married, and her popularity had been growing ever since. She had never willed this, and she couldn't stop it. Throngs of tourists gathered on her street for just a look at her. Day after day, she was deluged with baby presents from people she had never met. Even the hard-boiled Washington press was going soft for this charmed couple. They stood outside the Kennedy house for hours and days on end in bitter winter temperatures, waiting for they knew not what. One press-service woman described the aura: "We were numb with cold, but we knew we were recording a fascinating period in history, and from a privileged vantage point."

By Thanksgiving, Jacqueline was badly in need of a break from the hoopla, but she was unable to travel because of her close delivery date. JFK had the traditional holiday meal with his wife and daughter and then boarded a plane for Palm Beach to spend time with his parents. Jacqueline preferred he stay in Washington with her until after the baby was born, but he would not change his plans. When she walked with him to the front door, onlookers outside thought she looked like she had been crying.

But Jack was not going to get his vacation. Before his plane ever reached Florida, Jacqueline went into labor and delivered her second child, via cesarean, at Georgetown University Hospital. Everyone aboard Kennedy's private plane shouted enthusiastically at the news. The President-elect had a healthy son.

Beside himself with excitement, Kennedy ordered the pilot to take him immediately back to Washington. Like most other fathers, he had his first look at his son through the nursery window. He couldn't have been more proud of John Fitzgerald Kennedy, Jr. To reporters he bragged, "That's about the most beautiful boy I've ever seen."

John-John was baptized at the hospital chapel, and once again Jacqueline was confronted with cameras against her will, this time while she was being wheeled in her wheelchair. She didn't like it, but managed a gracious smile.

While Jacqueline was recovering from her surgery, she began tackling the demands of being First Lady. The President-elect was choosing his advisers and assistants, and she would need hers. Inauguration festivities were only a few weeks away. That round of ceremonies, balls, and private parties was only the kickoff for four more years of the same.

Jacqueline realized that if she was going to be the focus of national attention from now on, she would definitely need her own official clothing designer. From the moment the election results were announced, New York's Seventh Avenue fashion circuit was bubbling with speculation. Would Mrs. Kennedy choose to work with several designers or only one? The name whispered most often was that of Dior, the famous French couturier. But it was another Frenchman, Oleg Cassini, who won the prized appointment. Cassini already had connections to the Kennedys, to East Coast society, and to Hollywood. The brother of society columnist Igor Cassini, Oleg had once been married to Gene Tierney and had dressed Rita Hayworth and Grace Kelly. More importantly, he was a friend and supporter of JFK and had designed evening wear for Jack's mother and sisters.

While Jacqueline was still in the hospital, Cassini visited her and showed her sketch after sketch of ideas for inauguration dresses. She loved each one. But what she appreciated even more was his overall approach to designing for the First Lady. Oleg believed that Jacqueline's wardrobe should make a statement about the Kennedy administration and the nation, just as her husband's policies would. Jacqueline had already been selected to the World's Best Dressed list for 1960, and she was pregnant most of that time. If she could dress so impressively on her own, she might do even better with the help of this talented man. They liked one another right away, and more to the point, they understood one another. Jacqueline hired him on the spot. In less than eight weeks he would turn out dresses that would make her the sensation of the inauguration.

As soon as Jacqueline was released from the hospital, she had another task to face—the traditional White House tour given by the outgoing First Lady to the incoming First Lady. Jacqueline and Mamie Eisenhower had never had much contact or been fond of one another, and so neither of them looked forward to the day. The tour lasted only an hour and covered primarily the private quarters—the thirty rooms the Kennedy family would actually live in. After Mamie gave Jacqueline her tips on how to best run the place, the women stood before photographers for a few minutes, then Jacqueline headed back to Georgetown.

Before she arrived home, Jacqueline had made up her mind to make some changes; the White

House, for all its fame, would not be a very hospitable place to live if she didn't. She had found it cold, dark, and badly decorated, with a stiff, institutional feeling. If she accomplished only one thing in the next four years, she would refurbish and restore the White House to a building worthy of its great name.

Inauguration Day dawned cold even for January. The audience members who massed around the rotunda of the Capitol were bundled in their warmest dress attire, many of the women in furs. Most of them were cold indeed, but hardly seemed to care. For before them stood a young man and woman, a striking couple in any setting, but here, now, the new leaders of the world. Jacqueline was the only woman on the inaugural platform not wrapped in a fur. In pure and simple elegance, she stood apart in her her light wool coat, matching pillbox hat, and high-heeled boots. She was center stage, where she was born to be.

With the crowd of spectators, Jacqueline listened to her husband's inaugural address. It was the shortest speech of its kind on record, and one of the nations's most glorious. No one appreciated it more than Jacqueline, who said, "...it was so pure and beautiful and soaring that I knew I was hearing something great... it will go down in history... with the Gettysburg Address."

She was so deeply affected by what she had heard that, when he had finished, she could barely speak. True to her gracious style, she lightly touched his cheek and said exactly what she felt: "Jack, you were so wonderful!"

After the historic high point of the day came the social highlights. First there was a luncheon inside the Capitol, followed by a huge parade up Pennsylvania Avenue. Then the President and his First Lady enjoyed their first entertainment in the White House—a reception for the Kennedy and Auchincloss families. With a short break and a change of clothes, Jack went on to a dinner party for some of his closest friends while Jacqueline prepared for the inaugural balls.

The famous Mayflower Hotel was the site of the first gala. When the orchestra began "Hail to the Chief," every head turned to greet the new President and First Lady. Gasps from the guests mingled with the music. There Jacqueline stood before them, in a white chiffon gown and white silk cape. At her neck she wore a dazzling strand of Tiffany diamonds. Even Jack, who was accustomed to living with this beauty, was taken aback at first seeing her on the staircase of the White House. He beamed, "Darling, I've never seen you look so lovely. Your dress is beautiful."

Jacqueline enjoyed the attention of the adoring guests, and so did Jack. This was his shining hour, and he was enjoying every second of it. As usual, he had a witty remark to sum up the moment: "I don't know a better way to spend an evening—you looking at us and we looking at you."

From one ball to the next, Jacqueline was a sensation equal to her husband. The dancing and the private parties with movie stars like Gene Kelly, Tony Curtis, and Janet Leigh continued well into the night. By two A.M., Jacqueline was exhausted. She knew to excuse herself when she was tired, rather than have the public see her fading energy. Leaving her husband to continue his celebrations, she returned to sleep in her new home—1600 Pennsylvania Avenue.

To the role of First Lady, Jacqueline Kennedy brought an entirely new image. From her first month in residence she was determined to be herself and do things as she saw fit, regardless of whether they had been done differently in the past. She appointed Pamela Turnure, an old flame of Jack's, as her press secretary. Pamela dressed in the

"Jackie" style and imitated Jacqueline's soft-spoken, discreet manner. She was only a few years younger than Jacqueline, and understood how Jacqueline disliked the invasion of the press. The First Lady's new White House policy was simple: "My press relations will be minimum information given with maximum politeness." If she worried about having Pamela working in the same building with her husband, it didn't show. JFK's old friend, George Smathers, was sure that Jacqueline knew the score and also knew how to win the game. He explained, "She figured, 'I'm going to make this so obvious and easy for you that you are going to be bored.'"

As much as possible, Jacqueline refused photographs of herself and children. She agreed to do a couple of major magazine stories per year and was happy to leave it at that. However, the press didn't lose interest. In fact, the more they were denied exposure to the President's family, the more desperately they sought every morsel of news. What was Jacqueline wearing today? What did she say to Caroline this morning? A *Variety* headline told it all: JACKIE IS UNDISPUTED TOP FEMME IN WORLD. An NEA press story shouted, "Not since Shirley Temple zoomed into international fame a quarter century ago has an American child [Caroline] received so much internatinal coverage in so short a time."

Jacqueline combatted the glaring attention every way she knew how. She ordered the Secret Service to remove film from the cameras of intruding photographers. High shrubbery was planted around Caroline's playground to give her privacy as she rode her tricycle and played with her pets. Jacqueline believed that she and her children had a right to a normal life, even in the White House. She complained, "Sometimes I think you become sort of a... there ought to be a nicer word than freak, but I can't think of one."

For Jacqueline, one answer to the problem of privacy was to spend time with her children away from the White House spotlight. The sanctuary she chose was a farm called Glen Ora in Virginia's "hunt country." The town of Middleburg had only 660 residents, and most of these were the wealthy gentry who also enjoyed privacy and riding the hunt. She and Jack rented the four-hundred-acre estate and visited there as often as possible. The horsey jet set, the likes of the Mellons and Du Ponts, accepted Jacqueline as one of their own, both in the saddle and at the dinner table. Jacqueline rode well, and looked dashing

Smashing debutante Jacqueline quickly captured attention on East Coast society pages. But her eyes sparkled most for her father, Jack Bouvier. He became the model for the men she has most loved in her life. *(© Morgan Studio/ Photo Trends)*

Little Jacqueline was very fond of animals but not always so enthusiastic about her mother, Janet. When her parents later divorced, Jacqueline blamed Janet for her father's departure from their home. *(© Morgan Studio/ Photo Trends)*

Jacqueline was never more beautiful than on the day of her marriage to handsome young Senator John F. Kennedy. Even Republican leader Joe Martin was duly impressed with the extravagant reception, which guests remembered for years. (© *Pictorial Parade*)

Both Jacqueline and Jack were delighted with their first child, daughter Caroline. Behind the happy pose, however, there were strains in the marriage due to Jack's hectic schedule which kept him away from his family. (© *J. Murphy/Photo Trends*)

As First Lady, Jacqueline entertained heads of state from around the world, including the Shah of Iran and his wife, Empress Farah. But no Empress's jewels could outshine Jacqueline's already legendary elegance. *(© Pictorial Parade)*

While at the White House, Jacqueline delighted in her official trips with her President-husband. In England, she was graciously received by Queen Elizabeth II and Prince Philip. *(© Central Press/Pictorial Parade)*

Mourning in white, Jacqueline and her children attended a memorial service for JFK. The young widow received support from her brother-in-law, Ted Kennedy, and from Prince Philip of England. *(© London Express/Pictorial Parade)*

One of Jacqueline's chief concerns as Jack's widow was to promote a JFK Memorial Library at Harvard University. Brother-in-law Bobby Kennedy was her confidant and advisor. *(© AP/Wide World Photos)*

When the world's most famous widow began dating again, the press recorded her every move. On a tour of Cambodia, Jacqueline was escorted by Former British Ambassador, Lord Harlech. Rumors ignited that they were soon to be married. *(© Pictorial Parade)*

Through good times and bad, Jacqueline's closest female friend has always been her sister, Lee Radziwill. *(© London Daily Express/Pictorial Parade)*

Jacqueline's second marriage, to Aristotle Onassis, was a celebrated scandal. The aging shipping tycoon gave her all that money could buy, but their love did not last. *(© Pictorial Parade)*

Always an avid reader, Jacqueline chose a career as a literary editor. She counts among her friends dozens of well-known artists and writers. Here she attends a literary event with long-time friend Maurice Templesman. *(© A. Scull/Globe Photos)*

Jacqueline worked hard to instill in her children a proper sense of their Kennedy name. Through the years she has remained close to her in-laws, including Ted Kennedy. *(© Brian Quigley/Photo Trends)*

Nothing has been more important to Jacqueline than her children, and her dedication as a mother has had great rewards. Upon Caroline's graduation from law school, Jacqueline celebrated with son John, Ted Kennedy and Caroline's husband, Edwin Schlossberg. *(© AP/Wide World)*

Jacqueline Bouvier Kennedy Onassis is the most renowned woman of her time. Married to the world's most powerful man, and then to one of the richest, she has borne historic triumphs and tragedies with equal grace and courage. Many around the world have tried to copy her legendary style but she remains today, as always, uniquely Jackie. *(© Cliff Lipson/Retna Ltd.)*

doing so, as *Time* magazine reported: "Mrs. Kennedy hacked on the dirt roads around Glen Ora, on paths cleared of snow on the farm...Riding her bay gelding, Bit of Irish, she wore rat catcher: brown boots, riding breeches, tweed jacket, and black velvet cap."

Even in the country, tourists and reporters tried to track her down. But Glen Ora's long, narrow, secluded driveway made the Secret Service's job easier. Jacqueline could have hours of undisturbed playtime with her children.

Try as she might, however, Jacqueline could not escape the attention completely. Jack liked publicity and would coax her into more meetings with the camera than she would have liked. In one amazing week, the First Family was on three magazine covers simultaneously: *Journal*, *GQ*, and *Photoplay*. The editor of the *Washington Star* was delighted with the effect the Kennedys were having on the city. "It's been great," he explained. "More people are doing young and human things."

Jacqueline was mainly interested in events. She loved the arts, and soon the capital fell into step. If Washington's political leaders had snickered at culture in the past, they didn't now. Opera stars and Shakespearean actors were invited to the

White House along with the world's leading musicians, like Pablo Casals. George Balanchine, Carl Sandburg, Robert Frost, and Leonard Bernstein were all welcomed to Jack and Jacqueline's table. The Kennedys made a point of attending the National Symphony and the Washington Ballet. A portable stage was constructed at the White House so that performances could be accommodated at any time. The movement to embrace the arts was due to Jacqueline, but her husband eagerly followed her lead, because he believed a great nation had much to gain from its artistic achievements.

Jacqueline also set a new pace in other ways. She did not like the title First Lady, and requested that her staff always address her as Mrs. Kennedy. Nor did she commit herself to pet projects of a political nature, as Presidents' wives typically do. Democratic leaders in Congress urged Jack to have his wife more publicly visible, but Jacqueline held her ground about her privacy and her priorities: "If I were to add political duties, I would have practically no time with my children, and they are my first responsibility."

As in every other phase of her life, Jacqueline was first and foremost herself, despite the public scrutiny that came with living in the White House.

Each time she risked criticism by standing on her own, she actually gained more respect from potential detractors. Proudly, she admitted, "People told me ninety-nine things I had to do as First Lady, and I haven't done one of them."

Meanwhile, she took on the White House itself. Although it was a majestic structure on the outside, the interior was sorely lacking. The furnishings in many rooms were cheap or out of date and often in less than good taste. Throughout both wings, the decorating was in a catchall style reflecting the likes of the many different couples who had lived in the house before the Kennedys.

Jacqueline began the mammoth project by studying everything she could find that had ever been written about the great building. Since the White House had so much historic importance, she believed it should serve as a home not only to the First Family, but to the art and artifacts of the important times in American history. Perfectionist that she was, she wanted every acquisition to be authentic and correct, and she worked passionately to achieve this. She admitted, "I would write fifty letters to fifty museum curators if I could bring Andrew Jackson's inkwell home."

In order to tap the country's best expertise, Jacqueline appointed two committees to work with her on the awesome task, one to specialize in antiques and the other to oversee paintings and sculptures. JFK worried that the redecorating might be unpopular with the public because of the cost, so Jacqueline decided to raise all the funds privately—thus, it was a gift of sorts from herself and her friends to the nation.

Members of the committees and their assistants began a months-long scouring of the country, state by state, in search of valuable Americana. With the treasures they uncovered, Jacqueline steadily transformed the famous Red, Blue, and Green rooms from eclectic eyesores to regal spaces. The Green Room now reflected the federalist style of Thomas Jefferson, and the Blue Room, the French-influenced Monroe era. The 1830s' Empire style was displayed in all its gilt in the Red Room.

JFK was wrong about the public reaction to Jacqueline's efforts. Enthusiasm was the attitude in Washington and beyond, so much so that Jacqueline agreed to do a televised tour of the "new" White House for all Americans to enjoy. Forty-five-million people tuned in to watch her move gracefully from room to room, describing the background of each newly acquired art object. She relied on neither notes nor prompting, and yet she did not make a single mistake during the full hour in which she spoke in her whispery voice.

The television program was so well received that President Kennedy was himself very impressed. He not only appreciated her ability, but recognized that she was becoming a greater political asset with each passing year.

But it was not until their official trip to France in 1961 that he realized that her charm had swept the continent of Europe as well.

As soon as Jacqueline arrived in Paris with her husband, the city went wild. They called her *"charmante...la belle Zhakee."* Every move she made was reported in the press, right down to a change of lipstick. For the first time, she not only equaled Jack in popularity, she clearly surpassed him. Jack was pleased by the uproar over his wife and he characteristically joked about it to the Paris press club: "I do not feel it inappropriate for me to introduce myself. I am the man who accompanied Jacqueline Kennedy to Paris."

For Jacqueline it was a wonderful trip. She loved her ancestral France as the French loved her. Unlike her visit to France as a college student, she now entered the fabulous palace of Versailles as guest of honor. The elegance of the château impressed her beyond words. In turn, the French were equally impressed by her appearance at the banquet in the Hall of Mirrors. Her beauty was described as "Gothic Madonna" as she entered in a white bell-shaped skirt and a bodice of flowered embroidery under a white silk coat. In her hair, piled high à la Empire fashion, there was a spray of flame-shaped diamond chips.

Even the dour French President, Charles De Gaulle, was won over by Jacqueline. He called her the "gracious Mrs. Kennedy" and was duly impressed that she had read his memoirs in the original French. To JFK, De Gaulle enthused, "Your wife knows more French history than any French woman." President Kennedy had not anticipated this reaction, but he was pleased indeed. For some time, Franco-American relations had been chilly, and it was nonpolitical Jacqueline who was causing each side to warm to the other. De Gaulle was well-aware of the effect she was having. He commented later, "She played the game very intelligently. Without mixing in politics, she gave her husband the prestige of a Maecenas, which he would not have attained without her help."

During the Kennedys' state visit, De Gaulle made another remark, this one to his Minister of Culture, André Malraux. Malraux was taken with

Jacqueline, and she was equally attracted to him. Malraux made a quiet remark to De Gaulle about Jacqueline, and De Gaulle responded, "She is a star, and she will end up on the yacht of some oil baron." The French President could not have known how precisely he was seeing into Jacqueline's future!

Returning from France, Jacqueline had a new attitude toward her position as First Lady. Domestic politicians had never interested her, but foreign statesmen did. She agreed to make several state visits with the President, and in each case she scored important points for American diplomacy abroad. In Latin America she spoke to crowds in Spanish for her husband, addressing the plight of the underprivileged. She also took time to visit sick children at hospitals, and won their hearts with her smile and her assurances in their native language. These efforts were a positive force against Castro's pro-communist propaganda.

At the White House, Jacqueline graciously reciprocated her visits by playing elegant hostess to world leaders. She formed her own opinions about all of her guests. It was not the likes of the famous Macmillan or Adenauer that impressed her most, but rather, less renowned statesmen. She offered, "Two of the most interesting people were President Abboud of Sudan and President Kekkonen of Finland." And in her opinion, the greatest leader of all was not Nehru or De Gaulle but Lleras Camargo of Colombia.

The world over, leaders took a great liking to Jacqueline and bestowed on her lavish gifts. There was a leopard coat from Haile Selassie of Ethopia and a mother-of-pearl nativity scene from King Hussein of Jordan. When she received a diamond, ruby, and emerald necklace worth $100,000 from the President of Pakistan, JFK was quick to tease her: "You'll admit now there are a few pluses to being First Lady, won't you?"

By 1962 Jacqueline was feeling so diplomatically adept that she made a goodwill tour of Asia without the President. Her sister Lee, still her closest friend, accompanied her. The American and international press followed as she took in the glories of India and Pakistan. In Pakistan she was driven to the famous Lahore horse show in a golden carriage drawn by six steeds, and marveled at the Shalimar Gardens, which she found "even lovelier than I'd dreamed." She was equally amazed by the Taj Mahal in India, and studied the facade carefully both in daylight and in the evening. At Ghandi's memorial she placed flowers for peace, and in between sights she again visited a children's hospital and stopped at every bed.

After two years as First Lady, Jacqueline had clearly accomplished much for her country. However, in January of 1963 she was pregnant again and decided she would devote the year to her children. She instructed her secretary that all public activities should be suspended. Instead, she bundled up Caroline and John-John and took them for sleigh rides on the White House lawn, drawn by Caroline's pony, Macaroni. The threesome also went on picnics and to the amusement park, with the First Lady disguised with dark glasses and even a wig.

Soon enough, the nation learned that a new baby was due, and this genetrated more excitement. It would be the first child born in the White House in the twentieth century. It appeared that the First Family really did live in a special place like the Arthurian world of *Camelot*—the musical JFK so loved.

Jacqueline spent a happy, quiet summer at Hyannis Port with her children. But the spell of maternal bliss was shattered one day early in August when she went into premature labor after horseback riding. She was rushed to the hospital and JFK was alerted. By the time the President arrived, Jacqueline had given birth to another son, and he was immediately baptized Patrick Bouvier Kennedy. Mother was doing well, but the baby, who had serious respiratory problems, was not. It was decided that Jack would accompany the baby by ambulance to a larger hospital in Boston. Hour by hour the President watched his tiny child struggle to live, and he slept with him through the night at the hospital. But Patrick's heart and lungs were too weak to function, and he died the following day.

Friends like Cardinal Cushing had never seen Jack so emotional. He could not stop himself from crying as he made a public statement: "He put up quite a fight. He was a beautiful baby." Jack flew back to Jacqueline's hospital to tell her himself of the death of their child. He held his wife in his arms and cried, a gesture that stunned her as much as the news did. Later she remembered, "That was the only time I ever saw him cry. As shocking as it was for me, it was worse for him."

Still recuperating from surgery, Jacqueline was unable to attend the funeral. Jack alone carried his son's miniature coffin to mass. As a parting gesture to his boy, he placed in the casket the St.

Christopher's medal Jacqueline had given him on their wedding day.

Not long after the funeral, the Kennedys celebrated their tenth anniversary. In some ways, it was the best time they had known in their marriage. Although the death of a child can often drive a couple apart, the opposite occurred between Jack and Jacqueline. Jack made an effort to spend every weekend with his wife, and Jacqueline had a new sense of composure. When Robin Douglas-Home visited them, he noticed a difference in their relationship. "This tragedy brought them closer together than ever before, to a new plateau of understanding, respect, and affection."

Because Kennedy was now so sensitive to his wife's feelings, he was in a quandary when a phone call came from Jacqueline's sister. Lee was extending an invitation for Jacqueline to accompany her on a Mediterranean cruise. It would be a chance for her to get far away from the publicity in Washington, and could help her recuperate emotionally from Patrick's death. The idea of a vacation for Jacqueline appealed to both the President and the First Lady. The problem was the cruise itself. The host and yacht owner was a Greek shipping tycoon named Aristotle Onassis.

JFK worried about Ari's bad reputation in the U.S., both for his flagrant, illicit affair with Maria Callas, the opera star, and for his past indictment for conspiring to defraud the U.S. government with his shipping business. For the criminal charges, Onassis ended up settling out of court by paying a multimillion-dollar fine.

A further problem was the fact that Lee was currently having an affair with Onassis and wanted to leave her husband to marry Ari. After talking it over, Jacqueline and Jack decided she would take the trip. No doubt she could weather any negative publicity surrounding the association with Onassis, since she barely knew the man and would be only one of several guests on board, including Franklin Roosevelt, Jr., and his wife. Also, the cruise would give Jacqueline a chance to spend time with Lee and talk her out of divorcing her husband for Onassis.

For Jacqueline the trip was just the luxurious rest she needed. Onassis's huge yacht, the *Christina*, was stocked with the finest wines, caviar, and other delicacies flown in from Paris. The eleven guests on board had a crew of sixty to serve their every need, including a small orchestra for after-dinner dancing. While Jacqueline and her shipmates swam in the mosaic-tiled pool and dined on red millets and black figs, the *Christina* took them from one exotic port to the next: Delphi, Istanbul, Ithaca, and Crete.

Apparently, Ari was as happy to have Jacqueline aboard as she was to be there. Although they had an entirely proper relationship, Onassis made a show of his admiration of the First Lady on the last evening of the cruise. After handing out lovely presents to each of his guests, Ari stunned one and all by presenting Jacqueline with a diamond and ruby necklace that could also be worn as a bracelet.

Back in America, the press had reacted to Jacqueline's trip with questions of propriety, but the White House ignored the negative comments and the issue died away the minute the First Lady returned to Washington. President Kennedy and the children met her plane, and Jacqueline beamed at the sight of her family. Caroline bounded up the ramp with a clay bird for her mother that she had made in school. Behind the girl stood a smiling JFK. "Oh, Jack, I'm so happy to be home," she told him.

Feeling stronger than ever as a couple, the President and First Lady were more and more willing to support and help one another. So when Jack asked Jacqueline to accompany him to Dallas in

November, she agreed. The Democratic party in Texas was badly split, and JFK wanted to do what he could to repair things before the upcoming election year. He fully intended to run for a second term in 1964, and he wanted as much unity as possible behind his campaign.

This would be Jacqueline's first domestic political trip with her husband since he took office. She had never liked this kind of travel, but she knew how important her presence was to her husband. After all, she was the most popular woman in the country, and the fact that she was rather apolitical gave her extra power as a unifying force. To friends she explained, "Jack knows I hate this sort of thing... but if he wants me there, then that's all that matters. It's a tiny sacrifice on my part..."

Jacqueline packed carefully for the trip to Texas because she knew that what she wore would be a source of discussion and she wanted to be as impressive as possible without being overdone. For the three-city tour she selected two light-colored dresses and three suits, one yellow, one blue, and a pink Chanel suit that was fated to become indelible in the minds of many Americans for years to come.

San Antonio was the first stop. The Kennedys stepped off Air Force One to an excited, cheering crowd, and Jacqueline was presented roses with a card that read: "Respect and gratitude for your contributions to the cultural advancement of our country and to the image of the American Woman which you have carried abroad."

In Houston, the turnout for the President was even more impressive. An aide kidded JFK that "a hundred thousand more people came out to cheer for Jackie."

Fort Worth was the same story. Before dawn, an enthusiastic mob had gathered outside the Kennedys' hotel. After the President dressed, he went down to speak to his supporters. He realized that they were as interested in seeing Jacqueline as in seeing him. Joking, he said, "Mrs. Kennedy is organizing herself. It takes her a little longer, but, of course, she looks better than us when she does it... Why is it no one wonders what Lyndon and I will be wearing?"

When Jacqueline finally appeared in her pink Chanel suit and pillbox hat, no one was disappointed. She looked radiant as she greeted her fans and then went on with the President to nearby Dallas.

At Dallas' Love Field, a blue convertible limousine waited for the Kennedys and Governor John Connally. They would lead the motorcade to the

Trade Mart, where the President would give a luncheon speech.

The motorcade inched slowly along the Dallas streets as the President waved to the mass of supporters who lined the route. The sun was glaring, and Jacqueline was warm in her wool suit and wished she could wear her sunglasses, although Jack asked her not to. It was difficult to hear much above the din of cheering, but one thing the Kennedys noticed was that this was the first crowd they had encountered in Texas that waved negative signs as well as positive ones.

Jacqueline spotted a tunnel ahead along the route and looked forward to the brief coolness it would offer. But before they reached the underpass, an assassin took aim and shots cracked through the air. Both JFK and Connally were hit. For a moment no one, not even the victims, understood what had happened. Then Connally screamed. The President slumped toward his wife, and it was only then that she realized he had been shot in the head. Incredulous, Jacqueline clutched him to her, saying, "My God, what are they doing? They've killed my husband. Jack! Jack!"

During some of the longest seconds in history, members of the motorcade struggled to comprehend what was happening and to react. A Secret Service man hopped on the moving car and pushed Jacqueline down to protect her as the limousine driver gathered his wits and sped toward the nearest hospital.

Medical personnel were waiting when the President's car reached the emergency entrance. Reluctantly, Jacqueline turned her husband over to the doctors, but she realized there was little hope. As blood transfusions began, a priest was called in to give Jack the Last Rites. At her husband's side, Jacqueline knelt on the floor and prayed as he was pronounced dead. Slipping her wedding ring off her finger, she eased it onto Jack's hand, then kissed him good-bye.

To avoid the complications and delays of a Texas autopsy, the President's body was quickly placed in a bronze coffin and rushed to the waiting Air Force One for his final return to Washington. Amidst this most grotesque of tragedies, Jacqueline maintained remarkable strength and composure. On board the plane, she washed her face and hands and witnessed Lyndon Johnson take the oath of office. Her aides wondered if the emergency ceremony would be too difficult for her, but even in her private grief she managed to be courageous for the nation: "I think I ought to. In the light of history, it will be better if I was there."

When the swearing in was complete, Jacqueline left the Johnsons in the front of the plane and returned to her quarters in the rear. Still wearing her pink suit, now covered in dried blood, she repeated to Kennedy aides over and over, "What if I hadn't been there? I'm so glad I was there."

As Air Force One headed east to the capital, news of the tragedy spread to every city and hamlet in America. The nation had been cruelly, senselessly robbed of its great leader. John Fitzgerald Kennedy was dead. The days of Camelot were over. But the country still had one source of comfort and strength to cling to—Jacqueline.

# Chapter Five

*J*ACQUELINE KENNEDY HAD BEEN FIRST LADY FOR 1036 DAYS. SHE WOULD LEAVE IN THE SAME INIMITABLE STYLE IN WHICH SHE HAD ARRIVED. MOMENT BY MOMENT, SHE LED the nation through its greatest tragedy since World War II. She had left for Dallas a world-class celebrity. By the time her husband's casket was lowered into the earth, to some she was a legend.

When the news of JFK's death struck the country, schools and businesses across America stopped normal activity and watched in disbelief as the President's body was taken off Air Force One in Washington. Jacqueline walked off the plane with a grim but controlled expression, her bloodstained suit a badge of death for all of America to see.

Jack's brother Bobby, always one of Jacqueline's favorites, was immediately on hand to help plan the funeral services. The young widow wanted an historically proper funeral befitting her late husband's position, so aides in the State Department rushed to research the last great state funeral.

Plans came together quickly. The East Room was draped in black for a White House memorial service. On Sunday the President's body would lie in state at the Capitol rotunda, and on Monday there would be a funeral mass and burial at Arlington Cemetery.

Jacqueline also had to face the dreadful task of informing her children that their father was gone. Caroline was old enough to understand, and she took the news bravely, following her mother's example. Three-year-old John-John was less comprehending. When he was told that his father had gone to heaven, he asked, "Did he take his big plane with him?"

American families of every religious and political persuasion watched on television as the thirty-four-year-old widow led her two small children by the hand, following the caisson from the White House to the rotunda. There she knelt and prayed, as did the 250,000 mourners who filed through to pay their respects for the rest of the day and through the night.

At the same time, national leaders around the world made hurried plans to attend Kennedy's Requiem Mass at St. Matthew's Cathedral. Kings and Prime Ministers did whatever was necessary to reach Washington by Monday. It was not the United States alone that grieved, but the citizens of every continent. In all, ninety-two nations sent delegations to pay homage.

Jacqueline maintained strength at home as well as in public. JFK had once boasted, "My wife is a very strong woman." Grandmother Mrs. Auchincloss was always proud of Jacqueline's "marvelous self-control and discipline."

All of these qualities were on display in the private quarters of the White House where Jacqueline helped her family and aides bear their grief. As one long-time staffer later admitted, "Mrs. Kennedy carried us through...She kept so many of us from falling apart."

Others clearly followed Jacqueline's courageous lead. Shortly before the funeral mass on Monday, the CIA informed Charles De Gaulle that there was evidence of a plot on his life. Jacqueline urged the French President to drive to the church from the White House rather than walk in processional with herself and the international leaders. De Gaulle refused. He would walk in honor of John F. Kennedy, regardless of the consequences.

Once again, people around the world watched on television as the final ceremonies began. The multinational congregation of mourners marched with a black-veiled Jacqueline, Caroline, and

John-John the half-mile route to the church, each sad step underscored by somber drums and the haunting footfall of the riderless horse.

Throughout mass, Jacqueline maintained composure as JFK's old friend Cardinal Cushing led the prayers. At one point, the Cardinal's own grief was so intense that he slipped from Latin to English, saying, "May the angels, dear Jack, lead you to Paradise."

When mass ended, the funeral cortege left the cathedral for the last walk to Arlington, carrying the President's casket to one final rendition of "Hail to the Chief." It was then that the most heart-wrenching moment of all occurred. As the dress soldiers snapped to attention, Jacqueline spoke softly to her son: "John, you can salute Daddy now." Before the world, the little boy in the short blue coat and red tie shoes stepped forward and cocked his arm. Then Mrs. John F. Kennedy took hold of a torch and lit the eternal flame in memory of her husband. The Last Rites for President Kennedy were complete.

Shocked as humanity was by the loss of JFK, so it was uplifted by his wife's remarkable behavior. The Washington *Evening Star* said, "It has been as though she were trying to show the world that courtesy and courage did not die in Dallas."

And it was the *London Evening Standard* that perhaps best described the effect of the former First Lady's mien: "Jacqueline Kennedy has given the American people from this day on the one thing they have always lacked—majesty....She has taught the people of the United States that because they are the greatest power on earth, they now must assume the outward and visible signs of greatness—pomp and circumstance."

The country had said good-bye to one of its best-loved Presidents. Now it turned back to daily life. For Jacqueline, the adjustment was not so easy. In the period of just three months, she had lost a child and her husband. Next she would lose her home. For the White House had been personalized by her and it was where she had raised her young children and lived the happiest years of her marriage.

On December 6, 1963, there was a second kind of death felt by many Kennedy insiders. That early winter day, suitcases, bicycles, JFK's briefcases, and boxes of John's toys were all carried out of the White House as Jacqueline turned her home of three years over to Lyndon and Lady Bird Johnson. In the East Wing there still remained six-foot-high stacks of sympathy letters to be answered, 300,000 in all.

Just after noon, a limousine pulled up to the front entrance and Jacqueline, Caroline, and John-John left for their new, temporary home, a house in Georgetown lent to them by Averell Harriman. True to her considerate nature, Jacqueline followed through on the smallest details even on this sad day. For Mrs. Johnson she left a bouquet and a special note. She also took extra time to go to the Executive Office Building to say farewell to the White House operator. In the President's bedroom she left behind a brass plate she had ordered to be placed above the fireplace. It read: "In this room lived John Fitzgerald Kennedy with his wife Jacqueline—during the two years, ten months and two days he was President of the United States—January 20, 1961–November 22, 1963."

Thus Jacqueline Kennedy began her year of mourning. It was a lonely, agonizing year, but one she bore with grace. Her first reflex decision was to find consolation in the familiar. She said, "I'm going to live in the places I lived with Jack. In Georgetown and with the Kennedys on the Cape. They're my family." Toward this end, she quickly purchased a lovely Georgetown home for $175,000. For Caroline and John-John, she arranged to have the nursery-school children who had joined them for class in the White House now assemble at a private home so they would feel some continuity in their young lives.

She spent much of her time with Bobby Kennedy and others who were close to her husband. She now wanted to understand JFK's political life, which she had always avoided, as a way to stay close to him. Franklin D. Roosevelt, Jr. was one of the insiders she turned to, and he understood: "She makes it easy to talk about the President. She wants to hear everything about him. I think she realized, fully, from the first, what had happened...."

The first Christmas without her exuberant husband was a heart-wrenching one for Jacqueline. She and the children flew to Palm Beach to spend the holidays with the Kennedy clan, but no amount of family companionship could help her escape the void. However, she knew life had to go on, if for no other reason than her children's sake. Dressed in "summer mourning" white, the threesome did Christmas shopping along Worth Avenue, with John-John as always fascinated by toy planes and Caroline leaning more toward dolls. Christmas morning was the coldest on record, as the family without a father gathered around the

Christmas tree and the little boy and girl unwrapped a huge pile of gifts. For Jacqueline, too, there were thoughtful presents from those closest to her, and an unexpected surprise: King Hassan of Morocco officially offered her a vacation villa in Marrakech to enjoy at whatever time she might feel ready emotionally. "It is the least one can do to console such a brave woman," he explained.

In addition to her bereavement that winter, Jacqueline also had financial concerns. John left her a comfortable living, but she was by no means a widow of great wealth. Congress promptly allocated $50,000 a year for an office and staff. Her widow's pension would be $10,000 annually. From Jack's estate she received $25,000 in a single payment, $43,000 due the President from his salary and Navy benefits, and annual payments of $200,000 from a trust fund that Jack had set up for her and the children. Although the numbers looked substantial, given what she had become accustomed to, Jacqueline knew she would have to live within a budget.

As comforting as it was for Jacqueline to be in familiar surroundings, Washington was also a source of oppression, with its multitude of memories and its busloads of tourists who could be seen gawking outside her new home at any time of the day. If ever she needed privacy, it was now, and yet she could not escape the attention. "I'm trapped in that house and can't get out," she complained. "I can't even change my clothes in private because they look through the window."

Lee Radziwill was very aware of the problems her sister was facing, and she urged her to consider moving, perhaps back to New York City, which was, after all, their childhood home, and a huge city in which Jacqueline might not be noticed so easily. A friend told Jacqueline about a five-bedroom apartment on posh Fifth Avenue facing Central Park, where Jacqueline had often romped as a small girl. It offered security, privacy, and the selling price of $200,000 was manageable.

The move to New York was a good one, since it would give Jacqueline a fresh start and some much-needed anonymity. However, she missed her husband as much as ever, and her pain was one that nothing could assuage. "I can't believe that I'll never see him again," she said. "Sometimes I wake in the morning, eager to tell him something, and he's not there...religion teaches that there's an afterlife, and I cling to that hope."

It was the memory of Jack that Jacqueline spent her days and nights with. She did not want to forget him, and she was determined that the world should remember him too. What better way, she reasoned, than to secure fitting public memorials to JFK? At the time of the funeral, it was Jacqueline who had requested the eternal flame at Arlington. Then, before leaving the White House, she asked Lyndon Johnson to rename Cape Canaveral, Cape Kennedy. Johnson was happy to comply. Yet there was more to be done, she believed. She lent her support to the renaming of New York's Idlewild Airport to Kennedy Airport, and to the congressional bill to establish funds for a John F. Kennedy Center for the Performing Arts in Washington.

The project that she personally threw herself into was the John F. Kennedy Memorial Library at Harvard University, which would become home to some ten thousand objects associated with JFK. Jacqueline and those closest to her in the project conceived it as a place that would be lively and youthful, not just an institution "where the lights go out at five P.M." Recalling her happy college year at the Sorbonne, she wanted to imitate that atmosphere by making the memorial library a vital place available to students, faculty, and tourists alike.

A garden was another element that she considered important for the facility. The Rose Garden at the White House had been completely replanted under her supervision, Jack's favorite spot for a few minutes of respite from his demanding schedule.

So, with the aid of her dear friend and art advisor, Bill Walton, Jacqueline traveled the country in search of the right architect. She studied the latest renowned buildings and interviewed their designers. Always one to set rather than follow trends, Jacqueline surprised many by making an unexpected choice of an architect, as she had years earlier when she chose Oleg Cassini as her dress designer. A relatively unknown Chinese American by the name of I. M. Pei won the commission.

Although in succeeding years Mr. Pei would become one of the world's most famous architects and, among other projects, design the addition to the Louvre Museum in Paris, he was at the time stunned to be awarded the Kennedy Library project. Recalling that time, he said, "The day Mrs. Kennedy came to my office, I told her: I have no big concert halls to show you, no Lincoln

Centers. My work is unglamorous—slum-clearance projects...She didn't say much, but kept asking Why? Why? Why? about what I'd done."

Jacqueline had the education and innate sensibility to recognize Pei's great talent before he became famous. Walton explained her thinking: "I think Jackie, along with everyone else, liked him because he was low-key, genuinely humble about his work—and a man of Kennedy's own generation."

When the final decision on Pei was made, Jacqueline left the architect's Madison Avenue office and was confronted again with the reason why JFK memorials were so important. The lobby of the office building was jammed with people who had heard she was present, and even the traffic outside was congested by the curious. As she entered the foyer, the crowd went silent, then spontaneously burst into applause and cried, "God bless you!" Bill Walton worried that the scene was upsetting Mrs. Kennedy, but she assured him, "No, I'm all they've got left."

In different but equally successful ways, Jacqueline made a continuing effort to assure that her children retained a strong sense of their father. Although he was dead, she did not want him to be gone from their hearts or minds. She made sure they had "associations with people who knew Jack well and the things Jack liked to do."

Of course, summering in Hyannis Port was a key means of keeping the Kennedy identity alive for them. Caroline, who became quiet and somewhat withdrawn after the assassination, kept mementos of her father around her room. Bobby Kennedy spent as much time with the little girl as he did with his own children, since she seemed to brighten in his presence.

John-John's private school required that the boys wear ties, which pleased him since he got the chance to sport his father's PT 109 tie clip. Dave Powers, Jack's Irish sidekick, made a point of visiting John-John often, and played games with him as they had in the White House. Jacqueline pointed out to both children in what ways they were like their father. To John-John she would say, "Oh, don't worry about your spelling, your father couldn't spell very well either."

"Another part of knowing their father," as Jacqueline put it, was to have the children visit places that had been special to him. They went to Argentina, where John-John placed a small stone on top of the famous one his father had laid there. To educate them in their Irish heritage, Jacqueline took them on a month's tour of the Republic of

Ireland, including Jack's ancestral home in Dunganstown. To the press that awaited their arrival at Shannon Airport, Jacqueline said, "I am so happy to be here in this land my husband loved so much."

Jack had also loved politics, and in the same spirit of honoring the husband she had lost, Jacqueline gave her time and political support to Bobby Kennedy as a way to continue the legacy. Bobby decided to run for the Senate in New York, and Jacqueline offered to help the man who had done so much to help her. At Bobby's request, she attended the 1964 Democratic convention, where five thousand guests gathered to honor her former husband in a special reception. She also agreed to give an interview to the editor of the powerful New York *Post* to discuss Bobby's campaign. As the most respected woman in the world, people noticed when she spoke up. About Bobby, she said, "He must win. He will win...Or maybe it is just because one wants it so much that one thinks that...He is really very shy, but he has the kindest heart in the world."

People told her that time would heal. During the first two years after Jack was gone, Jacqueline asked herself and close friends, How much time?

Slowly, the answer revealed itself. There was no magic number of days. Rather, she gradually began to go out socially again, and even to have fun.

Photographers were ready to record her presence as she made appearances at a ski resort, or the opera, or a New York discothèque. If she wore white mink or a mint-green gown, it was duly reported. So were her escorts. At first the men on Jacqueline's arm were famous old friends who provided no threat of romance, men like Adlai Stevenson and Averell Harriman. Then more eligible men like film director Mike Nichols began to appear.

All of her adult life, Jacqueline's actions had garnered great public interest, and with it, gossip and speculation. Now that she was a single, dating woman again, rumors bred with incredible speed. Soon the press created its own list of likely future husbands for Mrs. Kennedy. One favored by the society oddsmakers was Lord Harlech. A former British ambassador to the U.S. and a recent widower, he visited Jacqueline in Ireland and accompanied her on a trip to Cambodia and Thailand. Certainly they shared the deep grief of those who have lost a beloved spouse. But from that bond, love did not spring. A close friend of Jacqueline's described the problem: "He's charming but he's boring."

Another escort often mentioned by the gossip world as a contender for Jacqueline's hand was Roswell Gilpatric, some twenty years her senior and three times married. When they traveled to Mexico together, they received widespread and unwanted publicity. Careful to guard Jacqueline's reputation, Gilpatric downplayed the idea of a love affair: "She's always been attracted to men as intellectual companions, as well as for other reasons. She is a person in her own right."

Jacqueline's family also watched her social calendar with interest and concern. Her stepsister, Janet Auchincloss Rutherford, explained, "Jackie wants to get married again because of the children. All the family wants her to...But we're afraid it will never happen...because anybody who married Jackie would be 'Mr. Kennedy,' and we don't think any man would want to do that."

Janet was wrong. There was one man seeing Jacqueline secretly who would never become "Mr. Kennedy." Jacqueline enjoyed his company and generosity and appreciated the attention he paid to her children. Because of his dubious reputation, she avoided seeing him in public, but they spent happy times together in her New York apartment. Aristotle Onassis, among the wealthiest men in the world—reportedly worth nearly a half-billion dollars—had his eye on marrying Jacqueline, one of the most famous women in the world.

But before Jacqueline could consider taking a new husband, she had a crisis of history to contend with.

# Chapter Six

*J*ACQUELINE KENNEDY COULD FEEL THE SWEEP OF HISTORY AND HER IMPORTANT PLACE IN IT. SHE LED THE COUNTRY IN DIGNIFIED MOURNING AND ARRANGED FOR GREAT AND lasting ways to memorialize JFK's name and his leadership. But there was one thing missing—a detailed record of the tragedy of the assassination, a sad but necessary legacy to posterity. Just as the former First Lady worked to ensure that her children would have lasting memories of their father, she also realized that, painful as it would be to herself and the nation, a history of November 22, 1963, must be written for the generations to come.

Bobby was willing and eager to execute the plan, and members of the New Frontier gathered under gray February skies in 1964, still deeply in grief but determined to proceed with the chronicle of the nation's darkest hour. William Manchester was the man chosen by Bobby and approved by Jacqueline to write the definitive story that would become one of the best-selling and most controversial books of the century. As a former newspaper reporter, and author of a highly flattering book about JFK, *Portrait of a President*, Manchester was an obvious choice.

Although Jacqueline had not previously met Manchester, she admired the writing she had read, and knew that Jack had been enthusiastic about his work as well. Emotions were strong and united, and the meetings were relatively brief because agreement came so easily. A short "memorandum of understanding" was drawn up, whereby Manchester agreed to withhold publication until five years after the President's death unless the Kennedys agreed otherwise, and to grant Jacqueline and Bobby a full review of the material before it went to press. In return, the Kennedys would give him full cooperation in his research.

Manchester was thrilled with the assignment and described it at the time as a "trust, an honor." So in those first bitter and lonely months of her widowhood, Jacqueline felt comforted in the knowledge that Jack's history was in capable and caring hands. Little could she have foreseen that her noble aims would result in a controversy that she would later describe as "the worst thing in my life," and that the publication of *The Death of a President* would also mark the beginning of the end of Jacqueline's position as America's revered celebrity/saint.

Manchester plunged into the work with a vengeance. Moving from his home in Connecticut to Washington, D.C., he began a schedule of sixteen-hour days, with few days off. His headquarters was an office in the National Archives building, and with the help of entrée calls and notes from the Kennedys, he launched a year-long series of exhaustive interviews with every person in any way remotely connected to the events surrounding the assassination. For months on end he faced one witness after another, many of whom "broke down right in the middle of the interviews." By choice, Manchester worked alone, transcribing his reams of shorthand notes and typing his own correspondence in an effort to give the history a singular voice.

Over and over he walked the streets of Capitol Hill, visited Arlington Cemetery, and even retraced on foot the course of the fateful Dallas motorcade. By his own admission, he became obsessed with the project. He had myriad questions that Jacqueline and RFK had neither the time nor the emotional stamina to answer. So a system of communication was established by which Manchester left his inquiries with Bobby's secretary, Angie Novello, who in turn did her best to pass messages along.

Of all the conversations that Manchester would record and annotate, the hours he spent talking to Jacqueline would be by far the most crucial. The historic value of her words was obvious both then and now. But her revelations were also the basis for the acrimonious "battle of the book" that neither of them could have imagined when the interview was conducted in private commiseration in the spring of 1964. For two days running, Manchester visited Jacqueline at her Georgetown home. He came alone, with only a tape recorder as a witness, while the very private former First Lady dropped her famous composure and for ten hours poured forth all the emotions she felt over the death of her husband. Sources close to the situation described it as so personal and sensitive that it resembled a psychiatrist's session with a patient.

Jacqueline herself later described the event to Joe Frantz for the LBJ oral history project this way: "I did my oral history with [Manchester] in an evening and alone, and it's rather hard to stop when the floodgates open. I just talked about private things. Then the man went away, and I think he was very upset during the writing of this book ... Now, in hindsight, it seems wrong to have ever done that book at that time."

Unfortunately, Jacqueline didn't gain hindsight

until some two years later. At the end of 1964 she was still one hundred percent behind the project, and let Manchester know it. He was invited occasionally to Hyannis Port and Hickory Hill, and in October of that year Jacqueline sent a letter to an author in which she described her satisfaction with Manchester, and went so far as to send Manchester a carbon copy: "I chose Mr. Manchester because I respect his ability... Many people will write of last November for years—but the serious ones will wait until after Mr. Manchester's book appears. This book will be the one that historians respect. What I am dedicated to is the accurate history of those days, and that will come from Mr. Manchester."

So strong was Jacqueline in her conviction, that she agreed with Bobby when her brother-in-law decided that a five-year hold on the book—making publication in 1968—would not be wise. That would be an election year, and Bobby already knew clearly that he planned to run for the presidency himself. He wanted to avoid any events that could appear to be cashing in on his brother's tragedy. With Manchester's willingness, the date for the book release was moved up to 1966 or 1967, depending on when it was ready. This new schedule was pleasing to Jacqueline in another way as well. Several unauthorized books on the assassination were planned or under way, and she was very eager to have the official history beat out those other authors, who were most likely writing their stories for commercial success and with dubious attention to the facts. In the last decade, the press had exploited her privacy and the privacy of her family too often. She was determined to protect Jack from such mistreatment now that he was gone.

Writing at breakneck speed, Manchester finished his thousand-page manuscript by early 1966. Jacqueline was pleased at his progress but could not bear to read the words that would cause her to relive the grisly days of November 1963. Once again she turned to Bobby to handle the editing-and-approval stage of the project. But Bobby couldn't face the pages either, and entrusted the reading instead to two aides, Edwin Guthman and John Siegenthaler.

Their first reaction to the book was positive, although they suggested changes of a political nature—mainly rewording passages about Lyndon Johnson that seemed too harsh. Manchester agreed, but the alterations made him touchy and apprehensive. Never a modest man about the book or his abilities, he believed that he should be the final judge of every word. He went so far as to say: "One wins only if he is prepared to sacrifice everything...to lay down his life rather than quit."

So the stage was set for a trying new drama when the impassioned writer confronted Jacqueline. The circumstances that caused the explosion came as a surprise to both of them. *Look* magazine offered Manchester $665,000 for the serial rights, many times over what any of them had planned on. By previous agreement, the bulk of the book's profits would be donated to the Kennedy Library, but the magazine money would belong to Manchester alone. Bobby received the news first and went to Hyannis Port to talk it over with Jacqueline.

As he might have expected, she became angry and upset. This seemed to be commercialization at its worst. She could envision the pictures and headlines on every newsstand, just as it had been several years before, and this time someone would be making a small fortune in profits. It was not turning out to be the history book she had conceived. "I thought it would be bound in black and put away on dark library shelves." She begged RFK to stop the *Look* deal, and he said he would try. And try he did. But Manchester refused to break his contract with *Look*, claiming he would be open to a law suit.

In the following months there were confused and hostile calls, letters, and meetings. *Look* magazine first agreed to postpone the release of the articles until January 1967 rather than as originally planned—on the third anniversary of the President's death. They also relented about the number of issues, reducing them from seven to four. Both changes were at the widow's demand. Then there was the matter of actually reading the condensed version. Jacqueline couldn't face the pages, and gave them instead to Pamela Turnure, who raised more objections. Rumors and exaggerations hit the press, while no official word was given by either side. All that was known was that the conflict revolved around two issues.

The first involved the still-negative portrait of LBJ, and this concerned Bobby greatly. Jacqueline was determined to back him on this in the same way he had always backed her. Furthermore, she worried about the public exposure of her deepest feelings during her darkest hour, revealed to Manchester nearly two years before. Leaks to the press continued, and day by day more stories appeared, speculating on the aspects of the past she most wanted to keep protected.

Then, there were the reports about the shooting itself, how Mrs. Kennedy had tried to reach for a fragment of the President's skull when he was shot and how she attempted to cover the head wound with the bouquet of flowers she held during the parade. At the Dallas hospital, she was rumored to have kissed her dead husband's instep and to have eased her wedding ring onto his hand by using vaseline. Even little Caroline was brought into the arena of morbid gossip. Stories differed about when and how she learned of her father's death and what her reaction was. As a six-year-old, she couldn't very well respond, but her mother was furious. This wasn't the recording of history, it was the most heartless invasion of a widow and child's private life.

Jacqueline was determined to put a stop to it. Through Bobby and her attorneys and agents, she pushed for changes, deletions, and postponements of the magazine material. The misunderstandings and cross-communications between the Kennedys, Manchester, *Look* magazine, and Harper & Row, the book's publisher, continued until time finally ran out. The presses were facing a deadline, and the Kennedy agents were refused more time to review the text.

One of the publishers involved referred to that

time as "the most trying and distressing one in a forty-year publishing career." Jacqueline felt just as strongly. At the end of 1966 her representatives announced that she was launching a million-dollar law suit over her invaded privacy and, more to the legal point, Manchester's breach of promise in refusing her and RFK a final and full review of the text in both magazine and book form. Manchester's reaction was that Jacqueline's timing was outrageous—the first installment of the serialization was already at press. But, in fact, Mrs. Kennedy's timing was superb. Her huge and powerful publishing opponents froze in their tracks. They considered the damage a suit could do, whether or not she won. After all, they would be seen as attacking the widow of a national hero, herself now a national icon. They didn't consider long before they gave in.

In late December, Jacqueline found the courage to sit down and read the important passages in dispute in the magazine serial. Beside her was JFK's former speechwriter, Richard Goodwin. Together they went over every painful sentence that Jacqueline felt should be deleted or rewritten.

One involved the grisly details of the President's wounds. Another centered on the conversation the First Lady had with her husband at the hotel the night before his death. It was their last private conversation together. Equally important was a letter from Jacqueline to Jack written in the happy last month of their marriage. While on a European vacation, she had written these heartfelt words to her husband: "I miss you very much—which is nice—though it is a bit sad—but when I think of how happy I am to miss you—I know I exaggerate everything—but I feel sorry for everyone else who is married." Manchester had quoted her words directly, and now they were only paraphrased.

Perhaps most important of all, Jacqueline won for her children the privacy she sought. The long, melodramatic description of Caroline's reaction to the horrifying news about her father was reduced to: "She cried." In all, there were a dozen such editorial changes involving 1600 words out of 60,000. Goodwin took the revised copy to *Look*'s chief, William Attwood, and after another full day of deliberations, the men met the anxious press. The changes Mrs. Kennedy had requested were made. The magazine's representatives spoke first and insisted that they had not really lost the battle of the book, since nothing of historical substance had been cut. But the fact remained that Jacqueline Kennedy had stood up to the press and gotten her way. Even as a widow alone, she had fought for her family and herself and she had won. RFK, too, was happy with the results. The harsh words about LBJ had been softened, and so, too, had his worry about the political damage the book might cause.

Watching from the sidelines was Harper & Row, the book's publisher. They understood quickly what Jacqueline's victory over *Look* magazine meant for them. It was time to accommodate Mrs. Kennedy. At first they had hoped to simply duplicate the changes that *Look* had made. But Jacqueline had more than that in mind. She demanded a full review of the manuscript and insisted that Manchester return the tape recording of their ten-hour interview as well as copies of letters she had given him. Leaving her representatives to work out the specifics, Jacqueline left for a much needed vacation to the Caribbean island of Antigua. Hoping to have peaceful play with Caroline and John-John, she found herself tailed and photographed by reporters even as she swam with her children.

It seemed that the more she sought quiet seclusion, the more it eluded her. The American public had been following the Battle of the Book with great interest and they were choosing up sides. For the first time ever the former First Lady's image was appearing slightly tarnished. Many people sympathized fully with Jacqueline, but others wondered what exactly she was censoring.

Manchester was quick to voice his complaints against the Kennedys, and in melodramatic terms. "Dust, blood, and sweat are extremely disagreeable, especially when they are inflicted by people who have been close to you. The arena is as merciless as it is cruel." To the *New York Times* he compared Mrs. Kennedy to "Marie Antoinette, completely isolated from the world by her courtier-advisers. For the first time I know what it is like to live in a monarchy." But earlier Manchester had been quick to give himself a royal designation in *Who's Who in America*, where he registered himself as "designated historian of Kennedy assassination by Mrs. Kennedy, March 1964."

Soon after her vacation, Jacqueline summoned all her strength and forced her way through the harrowing pages of the book manuscript. She indicated the passages to be struck or altered, and Manchester and Harper & Row complied. Then she withdrew her suit and the world waited for the arrival of *The Death of a President* in April 1967, three years after it was conceived. Knowing that the book's appearance on store shelves would cause a sensation, Jacqueline granted a rare interview to the New York *World Journal Tribune* at the end of March, upstaging the book by a week and guaranteeing that she would have an undivided audience for her comments. She explained what it was like to try to conduct her life amidst "the stares and pointing, and the stories... The strangest stories that haven't a word of truth in them, great long analytical pieces written by people you never met, never saw. I guess they have to make a living, but what's left of a person's privacy or a child's right to privacy?"

But in the end, the book seemed to take on a life of its own. Sales were tremendous, and parties on both sides of the battle line benefitted handsomely. At the time of publication, Manchester could already count on over one million dollars for himself, and by prearranged contract, the Kennedy Library at Harvard was sure to receive ten times that amount. The "best-seller of the century," as it was called, managed to eclipse all the sensational gossip that came before. Readers were gripped throughout the 710 pages that covered every harrowing moment of November 20 to 25, 1963. Despite certain shortcomings—mediocre prose, and thoughts attributed to participants that Manchester could not have known—reviewers judged the book to be powerful, gripping, and moving. *Time* magazine said: "But all [problems are] rendered comparatively irrelevant by his basic achievement, which was to assemble an overwhelming mass of detail—so much detail that the story becomes larger than life or death. For no one normally ever has that much information about any event, not even an event in one's own life...In the end, he molded his mountain of minutiae into a highly dramatized reconstruction of the tragedy."

The record was made, history was recorded. For Jacqueline, however, another history was beginning. Ever so gradually and subtly she was changing her relationship to the American public, and it was changing its view of her. Having shed her life of mourning, she was ready to live again. And this new life was one quite far removed from American politics and her image as the former First Lady beset by tragedy. She was prepared to cast off the mantle of her personal grief before America was prepared to let her go as their living memory of the Camelot years.

As she jetted between the U.S. and Europe, sharing fun with renowned personalities the likes of Truman Capote and Mike Nichols—as well as her then-favorite escort, architect John Carl Warnecke—her long-standing admirers started to turn on her. Former devotees now sneered like jealous lovers: "I don't think you can develop deep, deep sympathy for a grieving widow who spends half her time at Ondine's and...appears in a mini-skirt." Americans had been having a love affair with the beautiful, elusive symbol of their country at its best. But the pedestal they had her standing on was beginning to crack, and there would be a new kind of shock for the nation when it learned the name of the man to whom it would lose her.

# Chapter Seven

*J*ACQUELINE'S VICTORY IN THE BATTLE OF THE BOOK WAS AN IMPORTANT ONE. SHE HAD STOOD FIRM AGAINST THE FORCES OF PUBLIC SCRUTINY, AND WHEN THE DUST SETTLED, she was still the most admired woman in America. However, by the following year, that would change. A publisher's poll had shown that the single story that would sell the most papers among women would have a headline like JACQUELINE KENNEDY REMARRIES. A story about a world peace treaty would be the second most popular. In 1968, readers would get the story they most wanted but it would be a tale far different than any they had envisioned.

It was a time of turmoil and change for the country and for its leading lady, Jacqueline. Across the nation, college campuses were hotbeds of social protest. The war in Vietnam and civil rights were the biggest issues, and Bobby Kennedy, as a presidential hopeful, was deeply involved in both. In the background, Jacqueline stood ready to help her brother-in-law campaign by introducing him to influential people she had come to know. While the rest of the Kennedy clan threw themselves wholeheartedly into Bobby's campaigning, Jacqueline played her part much as she had with JFK —her mere presence at select events accomplished more than any number of hours of labor at RFK headquarters or stumping on the campaign trail.

But while Jacqueline lent her loving support, she also had grave reservations which she expressed to close friends. To one she said, "I hope Bobby never becomes President of the United States [because] they'll do to him what they did to Jack." No sooner had she confessed her fears, than an event occurred that greatly deepened them.

On a balcony in Memphis the civil rights leader Martin Luther King was shot to death. With sincere sympathy as well as political savvy, Bobby Kennedy responded immediately to the tragedy by flying to Coretta King's side in Atlanta. From there Bobby contacted Jacqueline, telling her that Mrs. King would very much appreciate her presence at the funeral.

Jacqueline had mixed feelings about the request. She had never met Mrs. King and she was a stranger to the black political movement. Also, the assassination brought back in clear detail the horrible events of Jack's death in Dallas. King's funeral would be traumatic for her, if only because of the difficult memories it would call forth. But Jacqueline felt a widow's empathy with Coretta, and she knew her cooperation was important to Bobby as well. So, bravely, she got on the first plane to Georgia. Mrs. King remembers her attendance gratefully. "She came to my house just a few minutes before the ceremony...She was very gracious. She said something about how strong I was and how much she admired me. I said the same thing back to her because I did feel that way."

Returning to New York, Jacqueline resumed her regular life, but there was a new addition to it that she was keeping under wraps. Aristotle Onassis, sister Lee's former lover, was seeing her more often. Although they had been acquainted for a number of years, the time they spent together now was frequent and intimate. Easter Sunday they enjoyed at a Greek New York restaurant, Mykonos, with Ari's daughter Christina and the renowned dancers Rudolf Nureyev and Margot Fonteyn. As spring bloomed into summer, they could be spotted together regularly at the Colony restaurant or Bailey's Beach Club in Newport, Rhode Island.

Gradually, those closest to Jacqueline realized that Onassis was not just another of her male escorts with whom she mainlained a friendship.

Bobby, particularly, guessed how serious the relationship was becoming, and it posed real problems for him. On a personal level, he didn't think much of Onassis. Years earlier he had been very concerned when it appeared that Lee might leave her husband for Ari. Politically, RFK wanted and needed Jacqueline's support, and that support depended on her untarnished image. No one with close association to the flamboyant Greek billionaire could remain untarnished for long.

At first Bobby tried to sidetrack Jacqueline in her new relationship by making jokes: "The Greek! He's a family illness." But Jacqueline countered that Ari truly meant a lot to her and was very good to her children. So they came to an amiable agreement—there would be no marriage plans made until after the presidential nominations.

The agreement, however, didn't stop the whispers among Jacqueline's friends and acquaintances. Many of them could not understand the attraction he held for her, and he was so unlike JFK that he seemed the least likely candidate for a husband. Not only was Ari twenty-two years Jacqueline's senior, but he was a foreigner and a man without any pretense of a social conscience. She seemed to be choosing a man just the opposite of her beloved first husband.

The reality was that Ari was both like and unlike Jack Kennedy. One friend, who was at first puzzled by Jacqueline's choice, made sense of it later: "...both were men of accomplishment, overreachers, heroes, if you will, and Jackie always had an eye for heroes...She had enough sense of her own strength...to marry a man of superior strength."

A former Kennedy aide agreed. "Jackie was at her best form with men at the top. They intrigued her enormously. She rose to great men just as she rose to great events." Several other friends viewed the relationship in terms of Jacqueline's childhood. They believed that she and Lee intentionally chose extraordinarily successful men as husbands as a way to make up for Jack Bouvier's failures.

There could never be any question that Aristotle Onassis was a success. He was not only one of the richest men in the world, but he had built his fortune single-handedly. His early life had not been easy, but he had treated every threat as a challenge and turned hardship into gain.

Born of Greek parents in Turkey in 1906, Aristotle was, by virtue of his nationality, somewhat of an outcast from the start. At age six his mother died, and the loss made an indelible mark on him, as Jacqueline's father's departure during divorce had made on her. Life tested and strengthened them both before they had left childhood.

When Aristotle was a teenager, new tragedies descended. World War I broke out and Turkey joined the Germans. However, Greece sided with the Allies, and suddenly the Onassis family, like many Greeks in Turkey, were viewed as the enemy. Aristotle's father was arrested and sentenced to die. It was only through his son's cunning and determination that he was saved.

First Aristotle befriended the occupying forces by securing liquor for them. Then he was able to persuade them to give him access to his father's bank vault. Before he was able to make prison bribes with the money, he was arrested, but soon escaped and immediately left for Constantinople. There he continued his efforts to raise enough money to free his father. He was still a boy, but he negotiated with his father's business contacts as if he were a seasoned entrepreneur.

In the end, he raised the cash and bought his father's freedom. For this sixteen-year-old youth, the lesson made its mark: Money equals life itself —the more money you have, the safer you are.

This, too, had a parallel to Jacqueline's childhood experience, when she was disinherited by her grandfather and her mother remarried a man who did not include her in his fortune. They both saw clearly that a person with money had a very different standing than a person without it.

The war ended, and Ari's father had his life and his freedom. But incredible as it seemed, the senior Onassis was actually angry with his son for the young man's remarkable efforts. He felt Ari had paid too much in the deal! Aristotle felt first stunned, then deeply wounded and betrayed. Years later, when his marriage to Jacqueline hit troubled times, he would feel the same way. Angry and defiant, Aristotle decided he would leave his family and cross the world to seek his fortune. He wanted to prove his worth, and he would spend the rest of his life trying.

He traveled in steerage to Argentina, arriving in Buenos Aires with less than a hundred dollars to his name. By working at low-paying jobs day and night and living below his means to save money, Onassis began investing in the tobacco trade, selling Turkish tobacco to Argentina. From these modest beginnings, he enjoyed profits that seemed to grow exponentially. Then he moved from trading goods to investing in the means of those trades—ships. Always using other people's money for investments, Ari began building a cargo fleet that would make him unbelievably rich.

Still, he was an outsider in Argentina, as he had been in Turkey. All his adult life Ari would cultivate the friendships of the most famous people in the world, in part because they interested him, and in part because he hoped to finally belong.

When Onassis turned his heart to Jacqueline in the spring of 1968, he had already been married and divorced, fathered a son, Alexander, and a daughter, Christina, and had enjoyed an infamous ten-year affair with the famous diva, Maria Callas. Only the previous winter, Onassis and Callas had finally agreed to marry. Then they had another in a long string of violent arguments and the engagement was called off. The man who now showered his attentions on Mrs. Kennedy was one who, at sixty-two years old, no doubt felt cut off from his family and lonely.

No one will ever know if Jacqueline would actually have risked the social breach and married the Greek tycoon if the forces of history had not struck once again across her path. Perhaps she would have dated Ari for a time, enjoyed his company, and then moved on to another companion, as she had been doing ever since JFK's death.

Whatever her intentions were, they no doubt were affected by a phone call on the morning of June 5, 1968.

Jacqueline answered the phone at three A.M. at her apartment in New York. Earlier she had gone to bed pleased at Bobby Kennedy's victory in the California primary. Now came news of another kind. Stas Radziwill, Lee's husband, was on the line saying the impossible—Bobby Kennedy had just been shot.

As she had with all the tragedies in the past, Jacqueline was able to quickly pull herself together and deal with the demands of the moment. She headed immediately for Los Angeles and arrived there while Bobby was still alive but unconscious. A team of neurosurgeons had done what they could, and all that remained was for Jacqueline to stand at Ethel's side and pray.

Their vigil wasn't a long one. When Bobby was declared dead, Jacqueline broke down and cried even harder than she had at Jack's deathbed. Perhaps she was feeling not only Bobby's passing, but that of Jack and her two dead children as well. Life seemed to deal everything to Jacqueline in spades—the blessings and the sorrows.

Despite her grief, she knew Ethel needed her, and she helped her sister-in-law with every aching detail that came with planning a funeral and burial. While still in Los Angeles, they began planning the ceremonies, and because the funeral music was very important to Ethel, Jacqueline made sure she had things the way she wanted them.

Jacqueline enlisted the aid of her friend Leonard Bernstein and asked him to arrange things as Ethel wished. That meant a Mahler arrangement and asking Andy Williams to sing "The Battle Hymn of the Republic." Ethel also requested that the nuns from her childhood be allowed to sing, although there was a rule against women singing in St. Patrick's Cathedral. Jacqueline stepped in and received a dispensation on this point from Cardinal Spellman.

The funeral mass was beautiful, and the sight of Bobby's children all dressed in white must have touched every person in the cathedral. There was deep sadness that day at St. Patrick's, but also a ray, however slim, of hope. Ethel had wanted it that way, saying, "If there's one thing about our faith, it's our belief that this is the beginning of eternal life and not the end of life. I want this mass to be as joyous as it possibly can be."

Jacqueline admired Ethel's faith, but she could not bring herself to feel joyous. Through all the years of her widowhood, Jacqueline had leaned on

Bobby as a strength and male support. He had helped her with finances and with giving time as a father figure to her children. He had always cared for her and rushed to be with her whenever there was trouble. Jacqueline had lost her father, her husband, and now her greatest supporter.

As the funeral train traveled from New York to Arlington Cemetery, crowds lined the tracks to wave a final farewell to RFK. Inside the train, people noticed that Jacqueline acted quiet and removed. She had been radically injured again, and she could not block the pain and the fear. Two Kennedys had been killed. What crazy person might attack a third? Her children were Kennedys. How could she guarantee that they would be safe?

The answer was Onassis. He had comforted her on his yacht when baby Patrick had died, and she turned to him again now. When the burial services were over, Jacqueline left for Hammersmith Farm to be with her mother and Hugh Auchincloss. It was not until she arrived that they realized that Aristotle Onassis and his daughter Christina would be visiting too. Jacqueline needed to be near Ari.

Jacqueline's mother was hardly pleased to entertain the unexpected house guests. She disapproved of Onassis not only because of his shady business dealings, but because of her daughter Lee's affair with him years before. She had encountered him in England and they had not gotten along.

Overall, the visit was very difficult. Janet was inhospitable to Ari, and Christina, too, did her best to make things difficult. For years she had been jealous of her father, never getting as much of his time as she wanted, and now saw Jacqueline as competition for her father's affection. Jacqueline's stepsister, Jamie Archincloss, recalled the entire scene: "When Onassis arrived, Mummy treated him very badly...But Christina was absolutely impossible to be with. Jackie was on her best behavior and tried desperately to get along with her, but she was just so difficult."

At the time, Janet believed her daughter was turning to the wrong kind of man for comfort. She didn't dream that they were close to marriage. But as the summer went by, Onassis spent more and more time with Jacqueline and with the Kennedy children at Hyannis Port. Gradually the notion rippled through the clan that Jacqueline intended to marry the Greek, even though she made no official pronouncement to that effect.

Of all the unexpected alliances, it was Rose who took most quickly to Ari that summer. They would spend time on the front veranda exchanging stories. She was not put off by his reputation for womanizing, because her husband had been the same way. He had been indicted on charges of tax evasion and investigated for questionable corporations, but Rose was willing to overlook these transgressions. She said later, "He was quietly companionable, easy to talk with, intelligent, with a sense of humor and a fund of good anecdotes to tell. I liked him."

Not everyone close to Jacqueline was as enthusiastic. Teddy thought a marriage to Onassis would harm his own political ambitions, but he was willing to support her in her choice. Andre Meyer, Jacqueline's financial adviser, disliked and distrusted Onassis. He tried, and failed, to change her mind. Her brother-in-law, Steve Smith, was also upset when he learned about Jacqueline's plans. He had political plans of his own and hated to think that association by marriage to Onassis might derail his ambition.

Perhaps most interesting and important of all was sister Lee's reaction. After all, she herself had wanted to marry Onassis, but reportedly never received a proposal. Without directly attacking Jacqueline's choice, Lee indirectly spoke against the union to friends: "I said to my sister recently—'I see no reason why you would ever want to marry again. You have already had everything, love, romance, and all that marriage can offer.' "

All of the Kennedys were also concerned about their Catholic image and the religious situation with Jacqueline's children. Technically, she would be in violation of church law if she married a divorced man. Jacqueline didn't want to give up her religion, but she didn't want to give up Ari either. So she paid a visit to Cardinal Cushing, the Kennedy family's longtime friend. She had always liked the Cardinal and felt close to the man who had baptized her children and led Jack's funeral service. She confided in him her loneliness and anxieties as a widow and told him how much better life was with Onassis. The Cardinal was sympathetic to this woman who had borne so many tragedies so bravely, and he assured her that he would support her marriage privately and publicly, although he had no power over the Vatican's decisions in Rome.

No one could dissuade Jacqueline, and even Caroline and John-John seemed reconciled, if not enthusiastic, about having a stepfather. One concern of the Kennedy clan was that Jack's children maintain their Kennedy and American identities. Finally it was agreed that the children would retain their Kennedy name and that they would both be educated in the United States, regardless of where Jacqueline and Ari might live.

As the only living Kennedy brother of his generation, Ted now stepped in to aid Jacqueline in the arrangements for her marriage. He was concerned that she and the children would be properly cared for financially by Ari. To secure the proper assurances, he had a meeting with Onassis aboard his yacht to work out the legal details of a new will for the billionaire.

Contrary to popular belief, Jacqueline did not marry Onassis for his money—although his wealth must have been a comfort to her, as it would be to any widow with two young children. Under Greek law, Jacqueline would receive a fixed minimum percentage of Ari's wealth at the time of his death. A second, larger minimum would go to his children. The figure for Jacqueline would have been $64 million. Because Ari's children were not happy about the impending marriage, he asked her to waive her legal right to the money as a way to appease his son and daughter. Jacqueline agreed, signing away the inheritance just as she had signed away her right to her grandfather's estate many years before. In exchange, Ted had Ari promise contractually to provide Jacqueline with

$3 million upon Ari's death, and to leave an additional $1 million to each of her children. Although the arrangement was financially comfortable for Jacqueline, the sum involved was not a great fortune by the standards of her society. Anyone privy to the facts could see that she wanted to become Mrs. Aristotle Onassis for reasons other than money.

By early fall, more people around the Kennedys came to realize that there was a marriage in the offing. Finally, on October 15, the secret intentions were made known to the world when a Boston paper took a chance on the rumors and printed a front-page story about an impending marriage between Jacqueline and Ari.

Jacqueline knew that public reaction to the story would be swift and probably harsh. To save herself and her children from a barrage of news speculation, she decided to marry as soon as possible. After a call to Onassis in Greece and another to her mother and to her sister Lee, she set the ceremony for the following Sunday. Then she arranged to hold a press conference. Through a spokesperson, Nancy Tuckerman, Jacqueline made an official announcement that she was indeed about to remarry: "Mrs. John F. Kennedy is planning to marry Aristotle Onassis sometime next week. No place or date has been set for the moment." Actually, the time and place were both decided on, but Jacqueline desperately wanted to have privacy in the chapel on the island of Skorpios on that very special Sunday.

Some of the Kennedy clan agreed to come to the wedding and others begged off. Jean Kennedy Smith decided to go despite her husband's protests, and Pat Kennedy Lawford chose to join her. Ted, however, claimed to be too busy, and the matriarch Rose also declined.

As expected, the press had a heyday with the news. The famous who had known Jacqueline were asked for their reactions. President Johnson offered "no comment." Bob Hope joked, "Nixon has a Greek running mate. Now everyone wants one." The Vatican issued a statement that Jacqueline was in clear violation of church law.

In papers around the world, Ari's character and Jacqueline's judgment were called into question. The press had done its part to create the legend that was Jacqueline Kennedy, and it seemed equally determined now to tear the legend down to erring, human size. The respected French paper, *Le Monde*, went so far as to say that Mr. Onassis was the antithesis of JFK's hopes for a better world. Through the outcry, a lone voice sided with

Jacqueline. Cardinal Cushing voiced his understanding: "All I know that I am able to tell you is this—*caritas*, charity."

Despite public opinion, the wedding day arrived with bright sunshine—the Greek sign of good luck. Two dozen guests filled the tiny chapel on Onassis's private island while reporters from around the world were held at bay by hired security forces. The most celebrated wedding of the century was intimate and simple. For the second time, Hugh Auchincloss gave Jacqueline away. This time she was dressed not in white, but in a beige lace Valentino dress. However, she was every bit as gorgeous a bride as she had been fifteen years before. The ceremony was traditional Greek Orthodox and lasted thirty minutes. John and Caroline stood beside their mother and new stepfather as the Archimandrite prayed: "Do Thou now, Master, send down Thine hand from Thy holy dwelling place and unite Thy servants, Aristotle and Jacqueline, for by Thee woman is united to man."

In order to satisfy and control the press, the newlyweds agreed to a brief photo session immediately following the ceremony. Then the entire wedding party headed for the reception on Ari's yacht.

Those guests who had not been aboard the *Christina* before were amazed at its opulence. They found million-dollar art treasures on the walls and marble throughout every bathroom. There was a screening room for movies, and even a mini-hospital in case of emergencies.

The celebration began with a toast of champagne, and then the bride and groom and all the guests retired to their respective suites to dress for the evening wedding feast. When Jackie reappeared for dinner, her guests were awestruck by her presence. Although they had all known her many years, she stood before them like a fabulous apparition. She wore a flowing white skirt and black blouse and gold jeweled belt.

But it was the ring on her hand that silenced the room. Her gold wedding band had been replaced by an egg-sized, unfaceted ruby surrounded by diamonds. At her ears dangled matching earrings.

At the dining table, the guests made more toasts and there were tears all around. Finally Janet Auchincloss made hers. To Onassis she said: "I know that my daughter is going to find peace and happiness with you."

# Chapter Eight

ON THE DAY FOLLOWING THE WEDDING, ALL OF THE GUESTS, INCLUDING JOHN AND CARO-LINE, RETURNED TO THEIR HOMES, AND JAC-queline began her life as Mrs. Aristotle Onassis. There was to be a month-long honeymoon in Greece, at least theoretically. In reality, Onassis had important business to attend to in Athens. This left Jacqueline with plenty of time to set her new house in order.

When Jacqueline became First Lady, her number-one priority had been to make the White House her own. Now, wife to one of the richest men in the world, socially eclipsing Elizabeth Taylor's marriage to Richard Burton, she set about remaking her new home in Greece. She summoned her New York decorator, the renowned Billy Baldwin, who responded immediately.

In Jacqueline's opinion, Ari's house on Skorpios badly needed redecorating and so did the yacht, *Christina*. Although a lot of money had been spent on making both places opulent, the decorating lacked good taste. When Baldwin got his first tour, he was taken aback by the ugly carpeting and the pervasive French-reproduction furniture. Onassis gave his new bride carte blanche on spending for the interior design, and with Baldwin's help, Jacqueline ordered over a quarter of a million dollars worth of new furnishings and art objects.

During this period, Jacqueline also contacted close friends whom she had ignored in the rush before the wedding. Perhaps the most important of these was her dear friend and former escort, Roswell Gilpatric. He had learned of her wedding secondhand, yet publicly and graciously wished her the best.

From Greece, she now wrote to him:

> Dearest Ros,
>   I would have told you before I left, but then everything happened so much more quickly than I'd planned...—dear Ros—I hope you know all you were and are and will ever be to me.
>
> With my love,<br>Jackie

Mailing off this innocent, heartfelt message, Jacqueline had no idea the trouble it would cause in the future.

By the time the redecorating was under way, the official honeymoon period was over and it was time for Jacqueline to return to the States to see her children. John and Caroline had always been Jacqueline's first concern, and they would continue to be so throughout her marriage to Onassis. From the start, Jacqueline and Ari led quite separate lives, with Jacqueline spending a great deal of her time in America and Onassis traveling wherever his business demands took him.

In the beginning, at least, this arrangement suited them both very well and they enjoyed the time they had together when they would rendezvous on the *Christina* or at one of their several fabulous homes—a villa in Glyfada on the island of Corfu, a penthouse in Paris, a hacienda in Montevideo, and an apartment in Manhattan, with over a hundred servants on call amongst the various locations. Ari explained their life: "Jackie's a little bird that needs its freedom as well as its security, and she gets both from me...She can do exactly as she pleases...And I, of course, will do exactly as I please."

One of the things that pleased Jacqueline was Ari's lavish gift-giving. More than once when he sent her flowers, the stems were cinched with a bracelet of diamonds. When she turned forty he presented her with a forty-carat diamond.

Although Jacqueline's life was far from staid,

she managed to give it order, as she always had before, to any situation. Holidays were spent with her children and her husband, usually in Greece. To make John and Caroline feel more at home, Rose Kennedy was usually invited to join them. Ari and Rose got along as well as ever, and Jacqueline found she liked her former mother-in-law better now than at the time she was married to JFK, because she could be herself without fear of Kennedy criticism.

Rose's presence also gave the children a sense of continuity and helped them feel better about being far from home on the holidays with a stepfather neither of them felt close to. He showered them with gifts, but they saw it as an attempt to buy their affection.

While Mr. and Mrs. Onassis and her children tried to establish themselves as a family, the international press hounded them, photographing their every move. Jacqueline and Ari were on center stage with their controversial marriage, and after the honeymoon, the attention still did not subside.

*Women's Wear Daily* christened the couple "Jackie O." and "Daddy O.," and the names stuck. It was not long before Jacqueline appeared on the covers of *Time* and *Newsweek,* while Ari continued to be criticized by the Western press for his lucrative business dealings with the oppressive Greek dictatorship.

The world remained intrigued by their lifestyle, their wealth, and their fame. Wearing furs or jewels, or lying on a beach wearing nothing at all, Jacqueline's image appeared in some magazine or newspaper, somewhere in the world, almost every day of the year. Onassis's villa in Greece became the best-known secluded sanctuary on earth. Demand for pictures of Jacqueline, her children, and her husband was so great that one photographer turned "Jackie-watching" into a full-time business.

Ron Galella was a paparazzo with great determination, ingenuity, and an appreciative eye for his subject. He had plenty of experience photographing celebrities the likes of Natalie Wood, Ali McGraw, Julie Christie, and Warren Beatty. But Jacqueline Kennedy Onassis held a special fascination for him, as she did for the rest of the world. "One word—challenge," he explained. "She's always trying to outwit me. Snobbish, cool... But how she can dress..."

In order to capture the photographic images that earned him thousands of dollars, Galella made a full-time occupation of charting Jacqueline's daily habits and travel schedule so that he could get the candid shots the public loved. He knew the days and times she visited her hair-dresser in New York and which plays she had tickets to see. For shopping, he followed her to Bonwit Teller, Gucci's, or Bloomingdale's. If she was riding a bicycle in Central Park with John and Caroline, he'd manage to be behind just the right bush to capture their activity.

Averaging an incredible one thousand pictures a year, Galella soon became known to Jackie as her special nemesis among all the press hounds. She learned to foil his efforts by ducking out of restaurants through the kitchen and hiding behind dark glasses, scarves, and flowers. In turn, Galella began to disguise himself so that he could continue to catch her unawares. He would wear wigs or hippie disguises, anything that might throw her off the track. At other times he would crash a party she and Ari attended by dressing in a dark suit and acting poised and quiet. It was always said of Galella that he never took a poor or unflattering picture of his favorite subject.

Soon he, too, was becoming famous—for simply chasing his famous subject. When an interviewer asked him why Jacqueline didn't give in and let him take the pictures, he answered, "Too smart. If she stopped ducking me, she knows the market on her would dry up."

In fact, it was Jacqueline's patience, rather than the market, that finally did run dry. At her wits' end, she eventually had him arrested in New York City for harassment. Galella responded by filing suit against her, charging "assault [for shoving him and breaking a camera], false arrest, malicious prosecution, and interference with his work." For damages, he asked for $1.3 million. Jacqueline promptly countersued, asking $6 million for "invasion of privacy and mental anguish."

At issue was Jacqueline's status as an international celebrity versus her rights as a private citizen. After six weeks of testimony, a Manhattan court ruled in Jacqueline's favor. Galella was ordered to keep his distance—fifty yards from her, seventy-five yards from John and Caroline, and a hundred yards from their homes and schools. Once again, Jacqueline had taken on a member of the all-powerful press and won.

But there was another kind of publicity Jacqueline couldn't beat.

Early in 1970 an unknown source stole letters belonging to Roswell Gilpatric from his office safe and sold them to an autograph dealer in New York. Four of the letters were thank-you notes from Jacqueline, including the fond note she wrote him during her honeymoon. Gilpatric quickly reclaimed the stolen correspondence, but not before the honeymoon note made its way into newspapers and magazines on both continents.

When Jacqueline learned of the violation she quickly made two calls. One was to Gilpatric to thoughtfully reassure him, as she knew he would be worried about her reputation. He said, gratefully, "She has been very understanding." The second call went to Onassis. Although she herself had done nothing wrong, she wanted to apologize for any embarrassment the situation might be causing him.

Onassis, who was known for his temper, reacted calmly to her explanation and assured her that he was not upset. Unfortunately, he was only masking anger which would erupt later. Whether or not Onassis believed the letter was more than innocent is not known, but the fact that Gilpatric was in the middle of a divorce from his third wife did nothing to soothe speculation. As for Onassis, it was the rumors and gossip about his young wife's possible infidelity that rankled him, attacking his old-world male pride.

Ari was known to be cruel when crossed, even to those he loved. He had always wanted freedom for himself in his marriages and love affairs, but it now appeared to him that Jacqueline had even more freedom than he—too much freedom.

To get even, Onassis made a point of seeing Maria Callas, his old lover and dear friend. They had had a terrible parting at the time of his marriage to Jacqueline, but Maria was so devoted to Ari that she forgave him and took him back into her life, giving him the friendship and understanding and passion he had always coveted from her. Their meetings were in Paris, in public, and the point was not lost on Jacqueline, who read in the papers that her husband was seen leaving Callas's apartment late several nights running. Quickly Jacqueline flew to Paris, and just as pointedly, had dinner with her husband at Maxim's for all the world to see.

The rift was repaired, but only temporarily. Onassis was beginning to complain to friends and associates about the wife he had loved to indulge. He criticized her extravagance and tardiness. Previously he had encouraged her to spend money on whatever she liked, and now he begrudged her what she bought.

Differences between them were becoming more evident. Onassis never read a book, and Jacqueline never talked to him about business. For that he relied on Maria Callas, as he had in years past. "She is the only woman with whom I can discuss business," he said. Jacqueline and Ari spent more and more time apart, and neither of them seemed to mind.

Perhaps the relationship would have mended slowly if not for a series of terrible events that played out like scenes from a classic Greek tragedy. The first involved Ari's only son, Alexander. As heir to the business dynasty, Alexander was beginning to have a place in his father's fast-paced world.

One suggestion Alexander made to Onassis was that he replace his aging Piaggio aircraft with helicopters. Onassis listened, but took no immediate action. In January 1973, Alexander made a training flight with a pilot on one of the Piaggio's. Just after takeoff, it malfunctioned and crashed. Alexander was injured beyond recognition and was taken to the hospital. After emergency surgery he was put on life-support systems.

Mr. and Mrs. Onassis left the States as soon as they got word of the accident. When Ari finally reached the hospital, he realized his son's massive brain injuries left no hope. He ordered the life support to be turned off.

Jacqueline was a veteran of sudden tragedies,

but this time she was uncertain of her role. Onassis was not only grief-stricken, but also tortured by guilt over the faulty plane. His extended Greek family surrounded him and indulged him in his mourning and self-pity. This Mediterranean display of emotions was far different than anything Jacqueline recognized from her stoic New England background. Naturally, she was sympathetic to her husband's pain, but it was difficult to make her sympathy felt amidst all the commotion. So she retreated quietly.

Onassis read Jacqueline's reserve as coldness. Bitter over the loss of his son, he began to lose his own zest for life. When Jacqueline and JFK had lost their son Patrick, they drew closer in their grief. This tragedy had the opposite effect on the Onassis marriage. Again Ari turned to Maria Callas for consolation. Certainly Jacqueline must have had some inkling of the meetings, but she chose to ignore them, as she had Jack Kennedy's extramarital affairs.

No doubt Jacqueline felt more emotionally separated from her husband with each passing month. Ari took his daughter Christina on an extended cruise without Jacqueline. Four years earlier Christina had been very unhappy about her father's marriage and in retaliation made a spontaneous marriage herself, to a Los Angeles real estate broker. Onassis was enraged by her hasty action and pressured her to get a divorce, threatening to disown her if she didn't. Now Ari worked hard to make amends with his daughter, his only remaining blood heir. Between them they agreed that she would be groomed to take over his business ventures.

In this way Jacqueline was further excluded. She had never been privy to Ari's business world, and her attempts to befriend the overweight, awkward Christina had failed. But things were not much easier for Christina either. She had never had a profession or much social confidence. Although she threw all her energy into familiarizing herself with her father's vast holdings, the pressure and responsibility finally overwhelmed her. While in London, she attempted suicide with an overdose of sleeping pills.

On the heels of this drama came word that Ari's first wife, Christina's mother, had died unexpectedly. Once more Onassis was sucked into a whirlpool of grief and anger. His former wife Tina's third husband was his own arch rival, Niarchos, who had also been married to Ari's sister, Eugenie. Eugenie had died under circumstances her family found questionable, and now the family wondered if Tina also had met with a bad end. This series of events left Onassis feeling cynical about marriage and about life itself.

The fiery tycoon was so despondent that his health finally suffered. While he and Jacqueline were in New York, he finally submitted to hospital tests to find out the cause of his slurring speech and drooping eyelids. The diagnosis was myasthenia gravis, a nerve and muscle disease characterized by weakness and fatigue of face and neck muscles. Managing the condition would require continuing, painful injections, but Onassis was assured that the illness was not fatal.

Despite Ari's unpleasant moods, Jacqueline did whatever she could to cheer and encourage him. In the year following Alexander's death, Ari had shocking business reversals, losing half of his total worth on paper. Understanding that her husband was under financial, physical, and emotional strains, Jacqueline suggested a trip, which she hoped would bring him rest and enjoyment. The place she chose was Acapulco, and no doubt she hoped it would be a kind of second honeymoon for them and bring them the happiness she had known there years before with Jack.

However, there was to be no rekindling of closeness between the couple. On the trip, Jacqueline suggested they might build a home in Mexico, and Ari became enraged and accused her of being a wanton spendthrift who had married him only for his money. She reminded him that, in fact, she had waived her legal claim to a percentage of his fortune at his request. What she said was reasonable and true, but Onassis was not in a reasonable state of mind. Before they left Mexico, he drew up a new will with language stating that he wanted her to inherit as little as possible.

When they returned to New York, Jacqueline went to her apartment, but Ari spent most of his time in a suite at the Pierre Hotel. Without informing his wife, he secretly contacted lawyers to investigate the possibilities of divorce. As always, rumors began to circulate and Onassis himself was the one feeding them by such tactics as having conversations with the columnist Jack Anderson. Jacqueline, for her part, remained poised and dignified. Through Nancy Tuckerman, her spokeswoman, she denied the possibility of a split.

As a young man, Onassis had a girlfriend named Inge Dedichen, who claimed that Ari beat her and was never sorry. According to her, he boasted, "Every Greek . . . beats his wife. It's good for them. It keeps them in line." There were never any claims that Ari had struck Jacqueline or Maria

Callas, but he surely had learned other ways to be cruel. He had turned against his first wife, then against his own daughter, and finally against the American wife he had formerly idolized.

Onassis didn't simply want a divorce from Jacqueline, he wanted to inflict punishment, because life had turned against him and he irrationally blamed her. By hiring private investigators, he hoped to find evidence of an affair he could expose. He found none.

Throughout this difficult time, Jacqueline remained strong by living her own life. She bought a fox-hunting estate in New Jersey, published an article in the prestigious *New Yorker* magazine, and gave immeasurable help to the successful crusade to save Grand Central Station.

By February 1975, Ari's bitter feelings got the best of him. In Athens he had a serious gall bladder attack. Jacqueline put his bad treatment of her out of her mind and rushed to help him. At her insistence, Ari was flown to the American Hospital in Paris for surgery.

Under normal circumstances, prospects for his recovery would have been excellent. But Aristotle Onassis appeared to have lost the will to live. After the operation, he never regained full consciousness or breathed without a respirator.

Initially, Jacqueline stayed at his side with the rest of his family. But the strain between her and Christina became too great, and Jacqueline began visiting the hospital for shorter periods each day. When she was not with her husband, she passed the time with friends in and around Paris.

As in New York, Jacqueline's everyday activities were photographed and noted with great interest by the press and public. If she were shopping on the Champs Elysées, went to a movie, hair appointments, or dinner with a friend, it would appear in the papers.

Christina was furious at the image of Jacqueline enjoying the city while her father was gravely ill. She didn't seem to realize that it was her own behavior, and accusations that Jacqueline had brought on all the family troubles, that kept Jacqueline away from the hospital.

After several weeks, Onassis seemed to improve, so Jacqueline felt she could fly home to New York to briefly see her children. Onassis agreed. While she was gone, Maria Callas came to the hospital to visit her beloved Ari. It would be their last meeting. A few days later, Ari contracted pneumonia and his condition deteriorated rapidly. Before Jacqueline could make arrangements to return to Paris, he died with Christina at his side.

Jacqueline was in Manhattan when she received the terrible news. Seven years ago she was a widow living alone in New York when Onassis came into her life. Now he was gone and she had come full circle.

# Chapter Nine

THE SHOCK OF ARI'S DEATH KEPT JACQUE-
LINE IN SECLUSION IN HER APARTMENT FOR
THE FIRST DAY. THEN SHE GATHERED HER
strength and headed for the funeral in Greece, via
France. When she arrived in Paris, she found that
all the funeral arrangements had already been
made. The Onassis family was icy to her, particularly Christina. They blamed her for not being at
her husband's death bed, and she saw no point in
trying to argue with people in grief.

In the chapel at the American Hospital, Mrs.
Onassis payed her final respects to the man who
had given her both happiness and pain. At the
young age of forty-five, she was already a widow
for the second time. She prayed at his casket but
did not cry.

Onassis was buried the following day in Skorpios, according to his wishes, beneath a cypress
tree near his son Alexander's remains. Ari's widow
and his daughter took separate boats to reach the
island, and they did not walk together to the
chapel gravesite.

Despite the sorrowful circumstances, Jacqueline

was chicly beautiful in her black leather coat and famous black sunglasses as she walked with John, Caroline, and Teddy Kennedy, behind the front line of the Onassis clan.

It was impossible for anyone to know what emotions lay beneath her controlled exterior. As *Time* magazine reported, "Her look was pure enigma."

One clue was a small bouquet of flowers that rested beside the grave with a card that said, "To Ari from Jackie."

Another was her statement to reporters following the service:

Aristotle Onassis rescued me at a moment when my life was engulfed with shadows. He meant a lot to me. He brought me into a world where one could find both happiness and love. We lived through many beautiful experiences together which cannot be forgotten, and for which I will be eternally grateful.

No sooner was Onassis formally interred than Christina began a battle of the wills. From the gravesite she went immediately to the *Christina* and claimed the boat and its crew as her own: "This boat and this island are mine. You are all my people now."

Before he left the island, Ted Kennedy tried to talk to Christina about the will, but she refused to enter a discussion, saying, "You better speak to my lawyers."

With that, the group of mourners disbanded to begin their new and very separate lives. Jacqueline headed for a vacation in France, Ted returned to the U.S., and Christina flew to Switzerland. From Manhattan, Lee Radziwill answered reporters' queries about her sister's future plans. She said, "I expect she'll come back here and carry on life as it was. After all, her children are settled here, she has her life here."

There was also immediate speculation about the amount of money Jacqueline might inherit. At the time of his death, Ari's assets included fifty tankers, Olympic Airlines, the island of Skorpios, his renowned yacht, and half of the Olympic Tower in Manhattan. Would the most famous woman on earth now become one of its wealthiest widows from her share in Ari's half-a-billion dollar estate? The press gave plenty of space to widely varying reports, ranging from $200 million to a paltry $2 million.

In fact, when the Onassis will was made public, the terms for Jacqueline were relatively meager. Ari left her $200,000 a year and an additional

$50,000 for her children, plus part ownership of Skorpios and the yacht.

Feeling this was an unfair bequest, Jacqueline's lawyers set about fighting for better terms. At first Christina remained adamant and would not agree to any sort of revised settlement. But after a year and a half of negotiating, a legal agreement was finally reached. Christina wanted to part company with Jacqueline permanently, and so the contract was structured around a one-time lump-sum payment. According to the terms, Jacqueline would give up her share of the island and the yacht and her annual allowance, in exchange for $20 million and an additional $6 million to cover American taxes.

During the year or more that the will was being settled, Jacqueline resettled in Manhattan. Her apartment on Fifth Avenue was once again her permanent home. She resumed contacts with old friends and old escorts.

This time Jacqueline chose not to undergo a period of official mourning. Instead, she decided to try something new, or rather, try something she hadn't done in more than twenty years. Six months after Onassis died, Jacqueline Kennedy Onassis made headlines again when she took a job.

Always ahead of her time, Jacqueline was a woman of the eighties even in 1975. To a close friend, she confided, "I have always lived through men. Now I realize I can't do that anymore."

As a great lover of books, Jacqueline was pleased and intrigued when her friend Tom Guinzburg offered her a position as consulting editor at Viking Press. Like many women in their forties, Jacqueline saw her children growing and becoming more involved with their own lives. At seventeen, Caroline was on her way to art school in London, and John was busy with his friends and his studies at Collegiate School in New York. The salary was a modest $200 a week, but for Jacqueline the money was not the prime consideration. She was about to embark on a career.

Although her salary was set at the going rate, Jacqueline's first day on the job was hardly typical. A photography session with the renowned Alfred Eisenstaedt was followed by an elegant lunch with the boss at the Plaza Hotel. Later, she explained her new position to reporters: "I expect to be learning the ropes at first... sit in editorial conferences... discuss general things... Really, I expect to be doing what my employer tells me to do."

What her employer expected was that Jacqueline would bring both her critical faculties and her social contacts to bear on the job. She would try to attract prestigious new writers to the publisher and give them editorial assistance through every phase of their projects. As Guinzburg admitted, "One is not unmindful of the range of contacts the lady has."

Friend and author George Plimpton saw from the start that Jacqueline had the skills to give her writers the attention they would need: "Jackie has the capacity of giving you the most extraordinary attention. She focuses on the person she is talking to with the most burning intensity."

The first book brought out under Jacqueline's editorship was *In the Russian Style,* a beautifully illustrated history of Imperial Russia's clothing and interior design. Not only was the book beautiful, but Jacqueline herself dazzled reporters at the publisher's press luncheon in her simple but elegant cashmere sweater and slacks.

Regrettably, not every project went as well. Jacqueline made the proper contacts, but for various reasons, Viking didn't follow through. After approaching both Lord Snowdon and Frank Sinatra about autobiographies, Jacqueline was disappointed in the way the men were treated. One employee remembered, "She nearly died the day she invited Lord Snowdon to lunch with Tom Guinzburg. Tom was very rude and disinterested in the memoirs. . . ."

Viking had financial problems as well. "There is never enough money to pay writers a decent advance. There's no sales promotion, no aggressive marketing," the former employee explained. "Jackie didn't know how to fight the company's sluggishness."

After two years with the firm, an event occurred which put an end to Jacqueline's association with Viking, though not an end to her editing career. The publisher released a novel called, *Shall We Tell the President?* By Jeffrey Archer. The plot involved Teddy Kennedy as the focus of an assassination attempt. The book was received to very poor reviews, including being described as "trash" by the *New York Times*. Jacqueline had not been involved in the project, but the reviewers, ignorant of the facts, treated the book as if she had and said she "should be ashamed of herself."

Jacqueline was not about to accept false blame. Instead, she decided it was time to part company with Viking. Nancy Tuckerman issued her statement to the press: "Last spring, when told of the book, I tried to separate my lives as a Viking employee and a Kennedy relative. But this fall, when it was suggested that I had had something to do with acquiring the book and that I was not distressed by its publication, I felt I had to resign."

Though Jacqueline's career was temporarily troubled, her personal life was quite happy. She was dating again, and naturally that was news, particularly now that her escorts were younger men whom she felt could relate better to her children. Her most frequent companion during this period was columnist Pete Hamill, six years her junior. The former live-in boyfriend of Shirley MacLaine, Hamill was a good-looking, engaging man of Irish descent who reminded some of JFK.

The couple was photographed continually, with captions asking whether he would be her third husband. Hamill had originally befriended Jacqueline by offering to connect her with potential writers for Viking. He also helped Caroline get a summer job on a newspaper. Once again, however, Jacqueline's romance was complicated by unwelcome publicity.

Years earlier, Hamill had written several critical columns for the New York *Post* about Jacqueline and her marriage to Onassis. When they were finished, he decided they were too mean-spirited to print and he filed them away.

Now that Hamill worked for the rival New

York *Daily News, Post* owner Rupert Murdoch decided to print the articles, to Jacqueline and Pete's great embarrassment: "Many marriages are put together the same way as the Jackie-Ari deal, although the brutally commercial nature of the contract is often disguised with romantic notions ...In a world in which men have most of the power and money, many women use guile, intelligence, or feigned submission to exist...."

Fortunately, Jacqueline was understanding of Hamill's position. After all, she had also been embarrassed by things written in the past and reprinted without her permission. He said, "She wasn't mad at me, but she was furious at that scumbag Rupert Murdoch."

Nor was she about to swear off the publishing world. Soon after leaving Viking, Jacqueline landed a better editorial job at Doubleday. The press turned out in throngs to record her first day of work, and she avoided them by showing up the following day instead. Doubleday was delighted to have her talent and experience and she settled quickly and comfortably into the position she has held ever since.

The staff liked her immediately. One editor recalled, "She dressed modestly and was given a ridiculously small, windowless office...She made it perfectly clear that she wanted to be treated like everyone else." That meant making her own photocopies and phone calls, although a secretary was assigned to answer her incoming calls to filter out any cranks.

A Doubleday in-house newsletter printed a short biography of their new employee that revealed much about how Jacqueline sees her current life and career. There is a description of her education, including Miss Porter's and her early work as an inquiring photographer, and then a history of her time at Viking—with no mention of her legendary life in between.

Jacqueline chose not to live off her past glory, but she remained close to those in her past whom she cared for, including Ted Kennedy. In his 1980 bid for the Democratic presidential nomination, Jacqueline gave her time to political rallies on his behalf. As one Kennedy staffer admitted, she was a terrific asset: "No doubt about it, she's the biggest draw. We reserve her for the big ones."

The big ones included rallies in Boston, New York, and St. Louis. One particularly impressive event was a gathering of Greek Americans at a Queens hotel. When she arrived, 1500 people chanted her name and clamored for her autograph. She hadn't lost her magic, not for a second.

One campaign aide put it perfectly: "She comes in like visiting royalty...People are thrilled just to get a look at her."

Twenty years had passed since Jacqueline had been through the rigors of campaigning with JFK, and her attitude toward stumping hadn't changed —she'd lend her help and her image by greeting people, but she didn't want to make any speeches. In the years following Jack's presidency, she had become no more political. At one Ted Kennedy reception an announcer said in error that Jacqueline would speak. Her reaction was instant and firm: "Oh, no!"

A Kennedy insider who witnessed the scene knew that a statement by Jacqueline wasn't necessary: "Jackie's presence *is* her statement." And the statement her presence makes seems to be one people never tire of hearing, or seeing. Even famous celebrities are thrilled to meet and associate with her.

In 1978 Jacqueline bought over three hundred acres on elite Martha's Vineyard, a Massachusetts island of retreat and pleasure for the rich and famous. Over the next three years, she spent another $2 million building and furnishing a dream house with the help of architect Hugh Newell Jacobsen.

From the moment she bought the very private property, the celebrity-filled island was charged with gossip. Jacqueline wasn't just another celebrity joining their private playworld. A legend was arriving, or even a myth. Was she everything they had read and heard? What was she *really* like? Was she building her own Hyannis Port compound? Or a castle?

By the time construction was finished in 1981 and Jacqueline was ready to move in, the island residents had at least some answers to their questions. The house, on the Gay Head section of the Vineyard, is a conservative salt-box design with an adjacent two-bedroom guest house. At first there were a few objections from neighbors over the thirty-four-foot chimney on the main house, which was taller than normally allowed. Architect Jacobsen came to Jacqueline's defense and won a zoning variance, explaining, "My client wants an upstairs fireplace because she likes to sleep on the second floor."

In true Jacqueline style, this home, which is the first Jacqueline has built entirely for herself, reflects her exquisite taste and sense of perfection without being overly opulent. At 3100 square feet, the house is large but not grossly so. The floors throughout the main house and guest house are a rich white oak. The windows are peg and groove, rather than nailed, a rare detail of superb craftsmanship. For entertaining dinner guests, the cooks have the help of a sixteen-burner stove, and every lovely bathroom offers a heated towel rack. Here Jacqueline has the home of her dreams and the seclusion to truly enjoy it.

Today, Jacqueline Bouvier Onassis, as she now calls herself, leads life exactly as she chooses. When she is not relaxing at one of her vacation homes, she enjoys a well-ordered routine in New York City. Three days a week she reports to work at her office at Doubleday, a short taxi ride from her apartment at Fifth Avenue and Eighty-fifth Street.

Her career demands are those shared by other successful editors. There are weekly editorial conferences, luncheons and meetings with writers, and a mountain of critical reading to be done at home.

Jacqueline's hard work, intelligence, and talent have made her a great resource at Doubleday. In the past several years she has produced a number of exciting and highly successful books, including her first best-seller, *Dancing on My Grave*, the troubled life story of ballet star Gelsey Kirkland. There was also the much-heralded collection of essays and interviews with the Lennons, *The Ballad of John and Yoko*.

More recently, Jacqueline managed to produce a book that everyone in publishing envied and no one believed was quite possible. Using her boundless charm and tact, she scored a publishing coup by coaxing an autobiography out of the sensational but difficult Michael Jackson. When *Moonwalk* arrived at the bookstores, there was a huge readership waiting eagerly.

The consummate professional, Jacqueline has moved quickly to her next great challenge—convincing the ever-elusive Greta Garbo to reveal her life in print. The deal isn't set yet, but Garbo is talking to Jacqueline, which in itself is an editorial feat.

Jacqueline once explained to writer and feminist Gloria Steinem why she so enjoys her career: "What I like about being an editor is that it expands your knowledge and heightens your discrimination. Each book takes you down another path. Some of them move people, and some of them do some good."

When Jacqueline isn't working, she may be found giving one of her well-known intimate dinner parties or enjoying Manhattan nightlife with escort Maurice Tempelsman, a diamond trader she has been dating seriously for several years. To maintain her enviable figure, she jogs regularly in Central Park and rides at her hunting estate in New Jersey. She also manages to find time to support landmark preservation projects, which have always been important to her.

A friend who has observed her life reports, "Jackie is in the driver's seat. She knows what's right for her. She leads a relaxed, controlled, uncluttered life."

Jacqueline has always honored her own priorities, and that is no doubt part of her success. Motherhood has always been more important to her than anything else: "The thing I care most about is the happiness of my children. If you fail with your children, then I don't think that anything else in life could ever really matter very much—at least it wouldn't to me."

Certainly Jacqueline has raised, singlehandedly, a daughter and son of whom she can be very proud. Caroline, thirty, is married to exhibit designer Edwin Schlossberg and has just completed studies at Columbia Law School. She shares her mother's natural beauty and unfettered glamour. Twenty-seven-year-old John is tall, dark, and very, very handsome, one of America's most eligible young bachelors. He received his law degree from

New York University in 1989, and now practices law in New York City.

Anyone who knows Jacqueline is impressed by her exemplary handling of her children. She sees them often and is as much a friend to them as she is a parent.

And now Jacqueline is enjoying the special privilege of being a grandparent. In June 1988, Caroline gave birth to a seven-pound, twelve-ounce baby girl, Rose Kennedy Schlossberg. Jacqueline is quite the doting grandmother, and has showered little Rose with gifts and attention, while sharing parenting advice with Caroline.

At age sixty, Jacqueline remains a world-class beauty, and part of the marvel of her good looks is that she is so very natural. One of her writers describes her: "She looks her age—little makeup, no facelifts—but she looks fine."

Of course, Jacqueline Bouvier Onassis is more than fine—she is a marvel, a living myth. She is gorgeous, graceful, witty, and rich. She is a serious and successful career woman and a model mother. She has been married to men of tremendous power and wealth, and managed to love and support them without ever standing in their shadows. She is able to enjoy the simplest pleasures of daily life, and also has risen to legendary heights during history's great and terrible moments.

She lives a life that almost anyone would envy. Once the world caught sight of her, it has always clamored to keep her in view. Her secret, of course, is uncomplicated but exceedingly rare. Jacqueline has never looked to others for how to dress, how to live, or who to be. She is, and always has been, an original. Jacqueline is simply Jacqueline, and the world continues to anxiously await her every move.

## About the Authors

Sam Rubin is a television entertainment reporter whose "Celebrity Sam" feature is syndicated internationally by Group W Television. He also appears on the "This Evening" program. Rubin lives in Los Angeles with his wife Julie.

Richard Taylor, a noted celebrity journalist, has written over seventy-five cover stories on many stars for a variety of newspapers and magazines. He is the author, along with Sam Rubin, of a biography of Mia Farrow. A native of Massachusetts, Taylor now lives in Beverly Hills.

# LANDMARK
# BESTSELLERS
## FROM ST. MARTIN'S PRESS

HOT FLASHES
Barbara Raskin
_____ 91051-7 $4.95 U.S.      _____ 91052-5 $5.95 Can.

MAN OF THE HOUSE
"Tip" O'Neill with William Novak
_____ 91191-2 $4.95 U.S.      _____ 91192-0 $5.95 Can.

FOR THE RECORD
Donald T. Regan
_____ 91518-7 $4.95 U.S.      _____ 91519-5 $5.95 Can.

THE RED WHITE AND BLUE
John Gregory Dunne
_____ 90965-9 $4.95 U.S.      _____ 90966-7 $5.95 Can.

LINDA GOODMAN'S STAR SIGNS
Linda Goodman
_____ 91263-3 $4.95 U.S.      _____ 91264-1 $5.95 Can.

ROCKETS' RED GLARE
Greg Dinallo
_____ 91288-9 $4.50 U.S.      _____ 91289-7 $5.50 Can.

THE FITZGERALDS AND THE KENNEDYS
Doris Kearns Goodwin
_____ 90933-0 $5.95 U.S.      _____ 90934-9 $6.95 Can.

Publishers Book and Audio Mailing Service
P.O. Box 120159, Staten Island, NY 10312-0004

Please send me the book(s) I have checked above. I am enclosing
$ _____ (please add $1.25 for the first book, and $.25 for each
additional book to cover postage and handling. Send check or
money order only—no CODs.)

Name _____

Address _____

City _____ State/Zip _____

Please allow six weeks for delivery. Prices subject to change
without notice.
                                                    BEST 1/89